SIEGE OF TITAN

MICHAEL G. THOMAS

First published in the United Kingdom in March 2011
This Second Edition published August 2011
by Swordworks Books.

ISBN 978-1906512699

Typeset by Swordworks Books
Printed and bound in the UK & US
A catalogue record of this book is available
from the British Library

Cover design by Swordworks Books
www.swordworks.co.uk

SIEGE OF TITAN

MICHAEL G. THOMAS

CHAPTER ONE

The seventh year of the war proceeded much as the previous six had. Though the Centauri Confederacy had reasserted control of Proxima Prime in less than two months, the insurgency was still underway. The fighting had moved from the plains and mountains and into the cities where technology and numbers counted for little. Every month the troop ships arrived and as they dropped off new recruits, the casualties returned on the very same vessels. The one thing that did change was that this was the first year in which the insurgents fought and held off conventional military forces in open battle. With their capture of the Bone Mill they were able to establish a strong defensive position up to a kilometre underground. It was the true beginning of their revolt and one that would see the Proxima System engulfed in the fire of crusade and holy war.

Reports of the Proxima Emergency

Spartan was hurt, really hurt. He hadn't felt this much pain in years and even then he hadn't been in danger of dying in such a degrading manner. As he lay on the ground he could feel the dull ache across his shoulder and chest from the impact, it took him superhuman effort to stay conscious. The arena floor burned his feet and as the pain kicked in his vision started to blur. He lifted his left arm and as soon as he moved the muscle he could feel the sharp pain in his ribs, it was like a knife being thrust deep into his flesh. He forced himself past the pain and wiped his brow, making him concentrate on the fight he faced. At the very least he had broken ribs and as for his shoulder, he had no idea. Anyway, it didn't really matter, as he was about to suffer far worse if he didn't move. He struck his hand against his chest, hitting the valve that released a dose of drugs into his bloodstream instantly numbing the pain in his body. In licensed matches these kinds of drugs were never needed but this kind of fight could lead to death, and in these circumstances he was more than happy to put something into his blood to give him a fighting chance.

Forcing his eyes open, he saw the dull metal mace heading for his head. With every ounce of energy he had left he rolled to the right. The weapon smashed down into the ground, missing his body by inches. He kept rolling and then forced himself up into a sitting position.

"Now I'm pissed!"

He dragged himself off the floor and up to face his

opponent.

Maximilian was his name, or at least, that was his fighting name. The man was massive, an image of a Greek god, he stood over two metres tall. His torso was puffed out with thick muscles and blood dripped from a gash across his stomach. Of all the opponents Spartan had faced, this one had caused him the most trouble. In fifteen minutes of gut wrenching combat they had both broken bones and cut flesh, yet they were still fighting.

Like all the combatants he had his own unique armour and equipment. He was armoured but not completely, as a fully armoured man was boring to watch. The crowd wanted to see mismatched opponents using skill and knowledge to best their adversaries. His lower were legs covered in titanium greaves, as was as his chest and shoulders. The metal gleamed with a dull iron finish and each plate was fitted with short studs that resembled spikes. On his head was a thickly armoured helm with metal plates reinforcing the sides and two rounded spikes that pushed out to make him look like an iron image of a hellish demon. The helm was the same colour as the rest of his armour and in the wrong light he looked like an armoured Minotaur of ancient myth. On his right hand he wore a studded metal gauntlet in which he grasped a dull metal maul. The gauntlet was slightly broken from the previous fighting but enough of it remained to protect the back of the hand and knuckles. The maul was a simple weapon but easily capable of braining a man or denting metal armour. It was solid metal and nothing other than an iron works would be able to damage it. On his left arm was a hexagonal metal shield with a runic symbol of relevance to him only, along with the symbol of a half-naked woman draped around the rune.

Spartan straightened his back, feeling the muscles and joints in his body clicking and crunching. For a moment he felt old but it was just tiredness and the pain of the fight. He moved his left leg forward into his fighting stance, much like a nineteenth century boxer. As he looked around the arena the bright lights made it feel like he was on some ancient desert battlefield. Sweat dripped from every part of his body and he could feel a trickle of blood on his brow. He looked down, spotting his weapon on the ground. Unlike Maximilian, he wore just one piece of armour. It protected his right shoulder and part of his chest but no more. It might look like this left him at a disadvantage, but without the helmet he had better visibility and wasn't bogged down by the shield and armour. Without giving his opponent time to stop him he reached down and grabbed his weapon. It was a metal rod about a metre long with a cast iron sphere welded to each end. It was crude but devastating when used by a strong man like Spartan. He grasped the weapon in the middle with both hands, a wide gap between each of them. He looked around, the bright glare from the lights still almost blinding him before he raised the weapon and gave out a roar.

The arena burst into applause and excitement as he turned to face all directions while keeping a wary eye on his opponent. This display was not just for the audience. He needed a moment to get his breath back. His ribs were making breathing difficult, without adequate air he wouldn't be able to match the machinelike technique and brute force of Maximilian. Even more important this display was annoying, really annoying, to the shield-carrying monster standing just a few metres away.

With a roar Maximilian had had enough and bounded towards him, his shield pushed out in front and his maul held high. It took just three mighty steps for him to get close enough for Spartan to put his simple plan into action. He dropped his weapon low and then swung it up and to his right so that it caught the lip of the shield. The mass of iron ball at the tip easily smashed the shield away from the giant, simultaneously exposing the monster's stomach. Spartan kept the weapon moving and brought the other end up high into his stomach, delivering a bone crunching smash. With speed and agility he leapt to his left and tilted his body just far enough away to avoid the maul and delivered another crippling blow against the back of his leg. With a groan the man crashed to the ground face first moaning in pain. A great cry burst out in the arena as Spartan raised his weapon with a pained smile.

"That's three down, two to go," he muttered to himself, the realisation that he still had more work to do hit him.

A siren blared followed by a muffled and crackling voice over a loudspeaker system. The lights flashed and then changed colour, bathing the area in a dark purple that transformed the mood to something deadly and sinister. Spartan hated it when they did this. It might impress the crowds but all it did was make his life much harder. It did mean that he had about thirty seconds before the next fighters entered though. He looked around, staring intently at the crowd above looking in awe at the savagery of the pit. All around the perimeter he could see racks of display boards, undoubtedly showing the latest odds for the scores of illegal gamblers that flocked there. They weren't the only people who came to the fights. Like the arenas of Rome there were many men and woman that simply adored the fighters. These modern gladiators had the same violence and virility that excited their ancestors thousands of years before. There were plenty who would pay good credits to spend a few hours with them after a major event like this one.

"Nothing changes." Spartan turned his attention back to the arena and the promise of yet another bloody spectacle.

With a shrill howl the siren announced the next fight was about to begin. At the far end of the arena a pair of heavy iron gates started to rise. There was no reason for them to be so slow and noisy other than that creating a further illusion of delay and suspense. This whole place was a pantomime of blood and showmanship.

The strobe lights flashed continually as the gates clunked open and his two opponents stepped out. As the first moved into the light a great roar went up through the crowd. Spartan knew immediately who it was. Keira! Nothing got the crowd worked up more than a scantily clad woman with armour and a weapon. She took a few paces forward so that she was standing directly in the beam of one of the main spotlights. She was tall, perhaps two metres and sported long green hair. She wore a folded metal skirt decorated with flecks of blue and gold powder to give it an expensive, unusual look. As expected she was fitted with a metal reinforced corset providing dubious protection, but it certainly appealed to the crowd. Of more interest to Spartan was her choice of weapon, an iron ball swung from a metal rod.

"Shit!" Spartan swore but not loud enough for the rest of the fighters to hear.

It didn't matter though as the second fighter had now arrived and for the first time he was faced with having to fight two women at the same time. She was much bulkier than the first woman. Her upper body and head were covered in exquisitely carved golden armour. He didn't recognise this one but the expensive armour made him wonder what was so special. Her legs were bare and for just a moment Spartan was distracted before he drew himself back to the fight.

"Come on, man, concentrate you idiot!"

From behind her back she pulled out two small objects that looked like half size maces. For a few seconds Spartan breathed a sigh of relief, until she shook them. With a sudden noise they extended to double their length and crackled with blue sparks. They were electro mauls and illegal outside of the police. They were potentially lethal, especially when placed near the skull or nervous system. Spartan had personally seen deaths in the arena from these weapons.

"Great, they never play fair do they?" Spartan laughed as he swung his own weapon in front of him and moved towards the two women.

The woman in the gold armour started moving the two mauls around her body as if in some kind of ritual dance, the other started to swing the iron ball over her head in a wide circle. The bright sparks flashed on the mauls, creating colourful lines and arcs as she spun them in a web of defensive patterns around her body. It might look pointless but he had seen this method before and it very easily confused and disorientated an opponent.

A loud blast on the horn indicated the start of the fight. Without hesitating Spartan moved to Keira and her circling iron ball. It was his intention to remove one of the women from the fight as soon as possible rather than have to fight both of them at the same time. He lifted his weapon up high, catching the chain connecting the weapons together. As they entangled he rushed in to strike her. He expected to hit her with the reverse end but before he could make contact the woman with the powered mauls was on him. The first strike missed but the second caught his left arm sending a sizzling spark through his flesh. It forced him to release his hand as he jumped back in pain. The weapon was obviously on its maximum setting so he had to be careful as it had the potential to confuse him enough to be struck by Keira. If they could both reach him this fight, and possibly his career, would be over.

As he staggered back she struck him again and again, each heavy impact numbed his muscles forcing him to his knees in pain. As Keira untangled their weapons the other woman moved up to stamp down on his head. It was his chance and with a quick movement he grabbed her ankle ripping it to the right. She lost her balance and collapsed. Spartan picked up one of her mauls striking her hard across the exposed parts of her body, the shocks sending her into spasms. He grinned and then remembered Keira. Instinct told him to move and as he jumped back he raised his newly stolen mauls above his head. It was a simple move he always made after a major attack or defence when he needed to recover to a safe distance for body protection. This was a lesson that early fencing masters had learned and it was a lesson not wasted on him.

It was the right choice as the iron ball came smashing down towards his face. The maul in his right hand took most of the impact but it still sent him flying across the arena.

"Keira! Keira! Keira!" The audience rallied behind the woman as she continued swinging the weapon over her head.

Spartan moved back and checked his weapons. The one in his right hand had stopped sparking, presumably damaged from the impact of the iron ball. The other still seemed to be working, just his luck.

Keira stepped closer, keeping the weapon swinging at just the right distance to threaten him but not too close to be entangled. Spartan moved and kept moving to maintain distance between the two fighters.

"Spartan! This time you're going down!" she shouted as she released the weapon.

The heavy iron ball rushed towards him and it was only with a superhuman effort that he was able to slide to the side to avoid the strike. As he regained his footing the ball swung back and she continued swinging it. She had developed a wicked technique that allowed her to both swing the weapon in wide arcs as well as to hurl it forward like a heavy iron cannonball from an eighteenth century warship.

He ducked and dived as the ball swung ever closer to him. His reactions were fast and it was almost impossible to strike him without leaving herself exposed. Then he spotted the opening. The iron ball moved just a little too far. He leapt forward past the ball and grabbed the chain. He could see the fear in her eyes. Then the lights cut out.

Shouting came from above in the crowd, though whether it was from missing the fight or feeling cheated at the prospect of losing their winnings he couldn't tell. Then the screaming started. Spartan stood still, as his eyes to adjust to the darkness. He could still make out the shape of Keira in front of him but little else. A flash came from above and several of the red emergency lights came on. They were low power but they did provide a dull red glow. He stared intently at the woman stood in front of him, they were both transfixed on their entangled weapons but the commotion above made it perfectly clear that for now the fight was off.

A loud blast echoed across the arena and the shape of a man tumbled down to the soft earthen floor. Spartan released his weapon rushing over to check him. As he approached a sickening feeling welled up inside. The body was a cop, but not just any cop. It was a man from the Advanced Tactical Unit. Spartan lowered himself down to look at him more closely. Like all ATU officers he wore the latest powered tactical armour giving them good protection. The armour also contained built in communications, analysis and air supply for riot duties. This wasn't the kind of gear a normal officer would wear, it was something you would expect when raiding an arms factory or for taking out a terrorist cell. What worried him even more was that he had two massive holes in his chest. Each was the size of his fist and neatly burned through the armour and out the back. The inside of the man was fused as though molten metal had been neatly poured into the wounds. The sides of the flesh were seared.

"Fuck!"

Keira ran over, examining the body before turning to Spartan.

"This man has been hit with a military issue thermal blast, probably at close range from a shotgun, you know they'll screw us for this?"

"Keira, what the hell do you know about military issue hardware?"

"Jackass!" She rushed over to the side of the pit. She moved fast, it was hardly surprising, he'd seen her move in previous fights and she was well known for her agility and physical prowess.

Two more bodies, this time from the spectators, dropped down into the pit. Spartan tried to move as a volley of shots hit the ground. It looked like they weren't taking any prisoners and in the open space there was no cover.

"You coming?" Keira called as she climbed up onto the metal gate and towards the lower edge of the viewing gallery. She dropped some of her armour down to allow her to move more freely.

More gunshots blasted across the site as extra ATU officers arrived and engaged in battle with whoever they were after. They could either stay in the pit and risk being shot or take the opportunity to try and get somewhere safer before any more of them arrived. Maybe they were after the gamblers or whoever ran the illegal fights. Who knew? The one thing Spartan did know was that he didn't want to be around when they switched the lights back on. It was ten years with no parole for unlicensed blood sports. They might not be legal but if you wanted the real thing you had to go underground, it was only there that real weapons and cruelty could be shown in all their glory. More important to Spartan was that he only needed two more fights to pay off his indentured service and be free of the bastards. He reached the ledge to find a waiting hand from Keira. He dropped down and into the viewing area. There were several bodies on the floor with scores of people running and screaming as they made for the exits. Around the computer displays and gambling terminals no less than a dozen men with advanced weapons were holding back double the number of ATU officers.

"This place is a goddamned warzone!"

"No shit!" Spartan swore as he looked for a way out.

At the other side of the room and right between the violent crossfire was a small door to a refreshment area. From memory Spartan was pretty sure it led to a shuttle bay where they could probably catch a ride. From the main entrance more black-armoured officers arrived. These guys meant business and wore even heavier armour than the first batch. Every square inch of their skin was covered with a special mixture of metal and plastic that could stop all but the mightiest of weapons.

The defenders in the club didn't seem too bothered and they responded with even more fire. Sparks flew from the police armour as bullets, shells and armour-penetrating darts hammered into the group. The three at the front engaged their shields as a batch of extending plates popped up from their armour giving them bulletproof riot shields. Their arms and hands remained free.

Several of the gamblers threw themselves at the police as they desperately tried to smash their way through the line of armour to the entrance and safety of the street. It was useless, only an armoured vehicle could smash its way through.

Spartan watched this battle with a mixture of concern and fascination. He could see the police were going to win the engagement and he didn't want to be around when that happened. He needed to get out and fast. As if to encourage him to do something the chair next to him and Keira blew apart, the blast from one of the police weapons smashing it to dust. Keira ducked back, trying to keep down and away from the fire.

"Come on, we need to make it across!" Spartan made

to move.

Keira refused and kept her head down and out of the way of the firestorm. Spartan took a step forward before a flash shell landed near his feet. The blast was massive and threw him hard into the gambling terminals. As he tried to regain his composure he spotted a number of the police moving in on him. A flash came from one and he waited for what seemed a lifetime to feel the pain of the impact, but nothing hit him. Instead, a scream told him something terrible had happened.

Spinning around he spotted Keira falling backwards with a gaping wound in her chest. He staggered forward to reach her but one of the ATU officers grabbed his arm and forced him to his knees.

"Give it up asshole! You're coming with us!"

The man was one of the newly arrived heavily armoured officers. Either his attitude or his armour gave him the kind of arrogance that only those immune to prosecution seemed to have. Spartan had never been a big fan of the police and this man had really pissed him off.

"Fuck you!" The wounded gladiator grabbed the man around the lower body and lifted him a good metre from the ground. With superhuman effort he smashed the man down onto the gambling terminals in a great flash of sparks and glass.

More of the officers ran in as the gun battle continued all around. Lifting a chair he swiped the first in the face and a second in the torso. He was like a raging madman and even several shock mauls wouldn't stop him. With the first few down he rushed towards three officers that had just arrived and were drawing their firearms. With instinct, brought on by over eighteen months of gladiatorial combat, he rolled low and snatched a firearm from the first man. He was taken completely by surprise as he was disarmed and spent his last few seconds looking down where his rifle should be. As the other two turned Spartan blasted him in the chest.

The police firearms were a new design and created specifically to end violent situations quickly but without killing the subject. Normally they would use weapons like shotguns but there were too many fatalities. Even safe rounds such as the beanbag shells were just not enough to end a situation peacefully without harm to the victim or the officer.

Incredibly thought Spartan, the weapon did its job. Each trigger pull released a bright yellow flash propelling the new rubber based heavy slug round. It might have been classified as non-lethal, but the shock from its discharge must have broken a good number of bones as the man was propelled through the air. He fired several more rounds, as the man continued on his trajectory before he smashed into a pile of chairs and tables. Without breaking sweat, Spartan lifted the carbine-sized weapon high slamming it into the jaw of the second man who staggered back several metres before reaching the edge of the fighting pit. Spartan knew immediately that he was screwed. It was as if the entire world was slowing down as the officer almost wanted to fall over the edge. He tried to grab him but another officer slammed a weapon into his stomach forcing him to the floor. The last thing he saw as a maul struck his head was the falling police officer tumbling over the edge into the fighting pit.

* * *

Spartan couldn't see. He tried to move his aching arms but they appeared to be lashed or shackled. He tried to move but his restraints stopped all but basic movement. There was a flash of light and his eyes burned with the pain of a newly born day. As he adjusted to the brightness he realised he was in a large room. All around him were scores of people in uniforms though no one was familiar to him. At the front was an overweight man in an official uniform who was flanked by several armoured guards. On one side was the bright purple banner of the Confederacy, the loose organisation that held the scattered fragments of humanity together throughout Alpha Centauri, Proxima Centauri and the old Solar System known as Sol.

The man, presumably the Judge, gave a signal and the room went quiet.

"I have heard the testimony and I am satisfied that

the evidence put forward by the ATU unit present gives a fair legal summary of the situation. Does the defence team have any additional evidence that is contrary to that provided by the ATU?"

Spartan, still dazed looked about the room for any friendly face. He noticed one man in a dark suit standing to draw the Judge's attention.

"Judge, if I may?" he asked formally.

The Judge gestured towards him and then sat down.

"The evidence brought against my client has not been proven. Yes, he was present at the site and, yes he was involved in the violent entertainment. Our main argument is that the ATU officers opened fire on the spectators and on those in the arena. It was a botched operation and by all accounts resulted in over twenty deaths, including six well-trained and equipped officers. It should never have happened and if the operation had been properly planned and executed, we wouldn't be here today. My client was simply caught up in a vicious exchange where he was forced to fight to try and escape with his life. Our plea from the start has been one of self defence and that is a right every citizen has in law."

"Nonsense! When a man breaks the law he forfeits his rights to due process, you will be well aware of the Citizens Charter! The ATU have provided video evidence of his culpability in the attack of many police officers and the manslaughter of Officer Riley, who was forced to his death in a terrible fall. This evidence was taken from the video feeds of every officer present. We have seen what was taking place. We are not talking about the usual televised combat sessions, this was unlicensed, murderous combat with weapons and equipment designed to maim or kill. Every officer who entered that building took a great risk for the public good and many paid the price," the Judge responded.

Spartan hadn't seen the footage, at least he didn't remember seeing it. But one thing was very certain. He knew a set up when he saw it.

"No way I'm getting out of this one," he muttered.

"Not only did the accused physically attack multiple officers present at the scene, he also managed to steal police equipment and turned it on them. We have the medical reports on the internal injuries and damage caused by his direct actions."

Some seated near Spartan looked at him, thinking they heard him speak but he just gave them a long hard stare. It was a hollow victory but it was something. The Judge continued.

"Based on the evidence presented, even after taking into account your argument of self defence, I have come to my decision."

It was a grim indictment of the way the legal system had evolved, in that Spartan's attorney just sat down and let the Judge continue. Spartan turned his head in disgust as he watched his rights torn up in front of his face.

"I have taken into account the difficult situation that the accused is in financially, but this desperation does not justify turning to illegal and dangerous combat. I am also convinced of the fact that the police raid was not initiated because of any specific actions of his. The raid was due to an undercover operation, that I am glad to report has resulted in over thirty arrests and the closure of six separate establishments, all of which were running the same form of gladiatorial entertainment. I believe him to be out of control and until he is properly re-educated, a man like this has no place in public and must be relocated to an area better suited to his character."

A murmur spread through the audience and cameras seemed to almost lean towards the Judge as they waited for the verdict.

"Based upon the crimes committed, the injuries caused and the death of a good police officer, I give Spartan two options and it is for him to choose one of them. Either he will face ten years for manslaughter and a following sentence of ten years for unlicensed gladiatorial combat at an unlicensed arena....."

Before he could continue, a volley of shouting came from the public gallery, as well as from the gathered press.

"Silence!" the Judge shouted as he brought down a heavy hammer that issued sparks across his desk. "I also offer Spartan the chance to redeem himself and his character by a term of service with the Interstellar Military. This term of service is to be no less than ten years and will involve a potential posting to countering the insurgency throughout Proxima Centauri."

He turned to Spartan and stared at him for several seconds.

"The choice is yours, Mr Spartan."

As the Judge sat down the two guards next to Spartan lifted him up so that he faced him. The attorney in the suit approached and stood to his right.

"I'm sorry, Spartan. We managed to get your murder sentence revoked but there is no way out of this manslaughter charge. We can go for the prison option and then go to appeal, but with the current waiting list for justice you could be in for two or three years before we could even consider going ahead. Alternatively the military option has risk, but based on your track record it could make you," he said apologetically.

Spartan looked around, he couldn't believe the situation he was in. Just a few weeks ago he was fighting for his life in a bloody arena just to pay for his mistakes years before. Indentured service meant he had to fight at twelve events and he only had two left before he was free. Now he was being offered a choice between prison or the military. He looked at the people around him and then at the Judge.

The room went quiet as everybody listened intently to his decision.

"You don't give me much of a choice," stopping as he gave the matter one last thought.

"You must decide or I will be forced to make the decision for you," said the Judge firmly.

Spartan looked around the room one last time. He would rather die than be forced to prison. Some might think his months working in the pit-fighting world were akin to prison, but he could leave anytime he wanted. He only stayed to pay his debt. It wasn't easy to stop an armoured-up, heavily equipped gladiator from leaving if he truly wanted to. He needed the work as much as the organisers needed him to fight. Twenty years would take away the best years of his life. By the time he came out what would he be able to do? At least with a full tour of duty under his belt he would have access to free education, state welfare, support and who knows, maybe even a career. He took a deep breath.

"I choose the ten years military service."

"Good, I am in no doubt that your skills will prove useful in fighting the insurgency!" he sneered.

"It is the ruling of this court that Spartan will forgo his sentence and instead offer himself for voluntary service in the Confederate Marine Corps for a term of service of no less than ten years. He will join one of the military recruitment transports where he will be transformed into a man the Confederacy can be proud of. The journey throughout the System is long but it needs to be. By the time you have made several passes through the sector you will be fully trained and capable of any military posting. It is an efficient system where you train as you travel. The Marine Corps is always looking for strong and resilient young men and woman to serve, and though this man has shown poor judgement he has proven an ability to stand firm and to fight when the situation demands it. A full term in the service of the Confederation will strengthen his character and mould him into a citizen befitting this fine society."

Spartan thought the Judge was now just enjoying himself with his little speech and was tempted to add his own thoughts to the proceedings, but the man continued with even more.

"It is of course assumed that to fully compensate the state for the damage he has caused he will give up a good and vigorous decade of training and service. If he fails to complete the full term for any reason, other than honourable discharge due to battlefield injury or similar, he will forfeit this verdict and be transferred immediately to a maximum-security prison to carry out the remainder of his sentence. Spartan, you will undergo two weeks additional medical assessment and care prior to your shipping to your boot camp. We need to ensure your injuries are fully healed before sending you on your way."

Spartan thought carefully. So, if he had an accident in training, faced a court martial or for any reason messed up, he could potentially find himself being thrown into prison.

"Case dismissed!"

CHAPTER TWO

The Personal Defence Suit (PDS) is the standard set of clothing, camouflage and tactical armour in one comprehensive package for use by CMC Marines. It can be easily augmented with a zero gravity manoeuvring pack or sealed for operations in limited atmospheres. It is lightweight and covers the entire surface of the individual. In trials, the armour has sustained damage from thermal and kinetic energy weapons and been able to operate even after sustaining over fifty percent damage. Variants such as the Combat Engineer Suit (CES) feature thicker armour, powered tools and augmented strength for use in the sapper role.

Equipment of the Confederate Marine Corps

Spartan stood in the departure lounge, a large hall where about a hundred new recruits were waiting for their various boarding shuttles to arrive. At one end were a variety of displays, some showed boarding times others news and information. Spartan wandered over, watching several of the people operating the displays. Like most public access points there were no buttons or screens to touch, the entire system was body driven and much like the combat training simulators he had used. A woman in her early thirties was running through various news stories on a large display. Using her upper body and hands, she moved and slid the stories as though they were stacks of paper or video files to play. Next to her a man of a similar age scrolled through a list of flights and was looking more agitated as he went on. Something caught Spartan's eye, it was live footage from the security feed. He looked down at the scrolling ticker text underneath about a suicide attack and it was coming from Proxima Prime.

"Oh shit! Have you seen this?" one of the recruits shouted.

Several more recruits wandered over to watch the details of the story. With a deft movement the woman enlarged the video and increased the volume. At the same time she slid over several more video feeds of the same event.

A man turned to Spartan. "Have you seen this shit? Apparently one of our compounds was hit last night."

"I heard they took out the wall with a suicide bomber and then stormed the place. According to the feeds the entire garrison was wiped out," said another.

Spartan looked at the video, saying nothing. The display showed a burning compound with a collapsed guard tower and several buildings still burning. Inside the base was an upturned armoured vehicle, one of the heavily protected transports used to ferry troops and supplies throughout the warzone. What really caught his attention wasn't the casualties or even the damage. It was the small section saying over a hundred weapons had been stolen. Spartan thought to himself, with those kinds of weapons they could attack and expect to damage or destroy any structure, person or vehicle in the area.

As interest in the story faded the woman flipped to another one. It was about the offensive to take the Bone Mill, a nickname given to the rocky underground mining complex owned by the Metallurgical Research & Mining Company on the northern continent of Avagana. Since being overrun by the insurgency spearheaded by the Zealots, it had been turned into an impenetrable fortress. He watched the report for a while, interested in the detail of a conflict he'd never really given much thought to. According to the article the underground research was invaluable along with the rich mineral supplies and the difficulty of getting people that far underground. From what he could see it looked like an underground hell that seemed to eat up marines. Based on the fact that he would soon be shipped off for combat, it might be an idea if he did a little homework beforehand.

From the information on the screen it appeared nobody knew why they were so desperate to hold onto the huge underground mining facility. It had originally been dug almost a kilometre underground to mine many of the precious minerals buried there. The resources were valuable but that had never interested the Zealots in the past. A year ago it was still operated by the state mining company, then something happened. Nobody knew what, but in days most of the crew had been killed and the place was taken over by more than a hundred Zealot fighters. By the time the military arrived their numbers had swelled to thousands and they were already sealing the access points to the structure. It was if they were trying to protect something very important. No matter how many marines the Confederation sent in, they were always repulsed and suffering heavy casualties.

The mining plant was built on the most recently developed landmass on the planet. Also it was where many of the Zealots had moved to in the hope of work and to avoid contact with the more urbanised area of the planet. It hadn't taken long for their extreme form of religion to burst into open revolt. When that was quickly crushed it turned it into the home of the insurgency. As well as scores of mines there were five major cities and hundreds of small towns and villages that had sprung up in the last ten years. In seven years the open countryside had become a wasteland with people staying in the urban areas to avoid moving in public where possible. Armoured convoys transported the workers and materials across the many roads and barely a day went by without hearing of another bomb attack on a major transportation route.

The Bone Mill had now taken on almost mythical proportions as the coalition had been besieging it for over ten months. The ticker said the total casualties in the battle had exceeded seven hundred and questions were being asked about the feasibility of securing such a formidable objective. With most of the access points blocked and thousands of metres of rubble making digging difficult, it fell to the marines and infantry to fight a slow, bloody battle as they claimed it one inch at a time.

He watched the screen a little while longer, there was an interview between two military experts about why the campaign was failing. The first, a woman in her thirties was looking agitated.

"Look, since the Zealots turned to terrorism we have been fighting a losing battle with extremists. Their numbers have increased each year, what are we doing to stop them?"

A man in his fifties wearing a smart brown suit grinned. "What are we doing? Well, since the start of the trouble the military has successfully repressed their capacity to wage war. They were only able to fight for a matter of weeks before they were contained and most of them were sent to the camps for trial." The woman interrupted.

"Rubbish, if we're doing so well then why can't we take the one place they have decided to fight for? The Bone Mill has been holding us off for months and the attacks on transports and supplies moving into the area are increasing."

"It is true the operation in the Avagana is challenging. But apart from insurgent bomb and suicide attacks we have the situation contained. When we finally take control of the facility the backbone of their resistance will be smashed and I can see the end of the emergency following shortly after."

"This isn't limited to just Avagana though, is it? We have had attacks in cities across Proxima Prime and the number of piracy and hijacking incidents off-world has increased. If you ask me I'd say the problem is spreading and at some point soon this local emergency could turn into a system-wide issue with long term implications," she added.

Spartan was getting bored and decided to head to the viewing gallery. The war, emergency or policing action, whatever they were calling it now seemed more complicated. He could see that the Zealots were extremists and the signs of their attacks on civilians across the Confederation were well known. What he didn't understand was exactly what the military were going to do about and more specifically, what they were going to want him to do about it.

He entered the observation area and moved towards

the windows. It was a round room about twenty metres in diameter projecting out from the main lounge. There were long comfortable chairs and Spartan sank down looking out into the blackness. The bright glow of the planet Prometheus below made spotting the stars almost impossible. Its black and red surface showing signs of the fiery hot surface, a place where only the most well prepared research laboratories and factories could survive, deep inside the solid rock. Not that it mattered as he was more interested in the light glinting off the ships that were moored and waiting.

The nearest vessel was a massive war barge, the CCS Vengeance. She was an old ship and had seen action in the first war fought in this system that had finally united the disparate colonies into one Confederation of mutually supportive organisations. At least that's how the history books reported a war that cost over three billion lives. Although originally classed as a heavy cruiser she was old and by modern standards outdated. She wasn't fast enough to serve in the line as a main ship but was still easily capable of moving at the speed of transports and civilian liners. She was still massively powerful and had been re-designated as a war barge, a vessel more suited to the slower work of escort and defence that was now probably of more use than the vessels in the main Fleet.

Since the start of the emergency she was one of the first vessels re-activated for use by the Confederation

Fleet to provide escort for the troop convoys. She was nearly a kilometre long with thick plate armour. What really caught his eye was the thirty-metre gash in her port side. Apparently a suicide bomber had steered a pilot barge directly into her flank and the damage would put her out of action for at least six months. Any other ship would have been lost in the attack, but not the Vengeance. Although she'd fought other similar vessels in the war, she had never sustained major damage, leading many to think of her as the luckiest ship in the Fleet even after the incident with the suicide attack. Over two hundred people were killed in that disaster. This had led to many people wanting to give the Zealots concessions. It was futile though, everything he had seen about the Zealots suggested they wanted nothing other than the spread of their idea of brotherhood. It sounded like indoctrination to him. Spartan began to wonder if enlisting rather than years in a cell was the best option for him. He turned his attention to another ship off to the right.

Through the thick glass he could just make out the shape of his new home waiting about three kilometres away. She was the CCS Santa Maria and from what he could tell she was hardly the flagship of the Fleet. The information pack he received on his enlistment said that fifty years ago the eight hundred metre long craft was a colony transport to move settlers. In more recent years, she had transferred to the Navy and refitted for a variety of military roles, the latest being marine training and transportation. Due to the nature of their deployment they would be on a journey of roughly two hundred and forty days before reaching their destination. Somebody had worked out that rather than spending half a year training recruits and then having to wait another half a year just to get them to theatre, this could be halved by doing the training on the way. It was an interesting idea and in theory was more efficient. What it didn't take into account was that not everyone would pass and be able to do their job.

"What happens if a thousand recruits left but only a hundred were able to serve as marines?" Spartan thought to himself.

Then he thought of the display on the suicide attack. It was simple really. Everybody would have to fight. They didn't have the numbers or the capability to return them home. In the end this deployment was a one-way posting. The only people going home were veterans and casualties, anyone else would be buried on the planet.

He looked back at the large grey vessel in the distance. She was one of over a dozen ships waiting on the outer pylons of the dock. The ship contained two rotating cylindrical sections providing an equivalent of Earth's gravity. The long cylinders were wrapped in thick plated bands at regular intervals. The middle section contained massive storage hangars originally used for raw materials and supplies intended for colony development. Now they carried military hardware and weapons, as well as housing a few dedicated zones for the dreaded zero-g training. Though not equipped for combat she did carry basic defensive measures against smaller vessels and missiles and a small amount of firepower from the gun batteries mounted on the rotating cylindrical sections. These were kinetic railguns but their effectiveness in action had never been tested.

As Spartan watched he could just see the multitude of tugs, shuttles and transports moving back and forth from the major vessels in dock. This place might be big but from what he had heard their destination drop-off point at the Titan Naval Station was much bigger. A shrill whine came over the tannoy system with the latest announcement. It was the message he was waiting for.

"Shuttle seven two nine is ready for departure. All recruits for the Santa Maria are to report in fifteen minutes. Please proceed to your shuttle."

With military precision the doors to the vehicle pool opened and glowing symbols along the wall indicated the path to take so that even the most dim-witted of the new candidates could find their way along the path to the waiting shuttles. As he walked along the path a trio of men pushed past, jostling to get to the shuttle first. One of them crashed into Spartan, almost throwing him to the floor.

"Hey!" Spartan reached out and grabbed the last of the

group by the shoulder.

"What's your problem, pal?" said the man with undisguised contempt as he tried to pull away. He was roughly the same height as Spartan and sported a neatly trimmed ginger beard and moustache.

"My problem is you." He straightened himself up prepared for a confrontation.

The other two men stopped and came to their friend's aid, standing either side of him. They were exactly the kind of people he expected to find here. Well built, probably college sports jocks sent away for a tour on the frontline. After one year's posting they'd come home and expect a cushy state job where everybody would crow over their service. The tallest, a man wearing a name patch of Burnett, stepped forward. He was almost a head taller than Spartan who was hardly a small man himself.

"Hey, Matt, this guy causing you grief?" He turned to Spartan.

He knew what was coming and also from years of experience you never, ever let your opponent get the drop on you. He also knew that a distraction was always a smart move for the first part of any offensive action.

"Burnett? Isn't that a girl's name?" he said with a grin.

The man was obviously used to being ridiculed, curled his face up in anger and opened his mouth as if to spout some clever line.

Spartan knew this was his moment and without

hesitation slammed his knee hard into the man's crotch. Burnett was taken completely by surprise and hit the ground groaning in pain. Spartan took one step back and lifted his hands so that his palms faced the group. To the untrained man it looked like he was worried or trying to plead with them. For anybody with knowledge of martial skills though they would instantly note the similarities to the basic training of systems like Krav Maga.

Matt, the man that had started it all took a step forward, sensing that Spartan wanted to avoid a fight. As he moved closer the number of people heading for the shuttles slowed as some of them stopped to watch the unfolding event. At the far end of the corridor a number of men in black body armour were making their way towards them.

He attacked, as far as Spartan was concerned he may as well have written down on a sheet of paper what he planned to do. He moved his feet first, instantly giving advance notice of his intentions. Then he made the classic mistake of pulling his arm back to deliver the strongest punch he could muster. He obviously lacked any real fighting skill and as his fist flew forwards Spartan sidestepped and pulled his arm from the side. He grasped the wrist from the back and put his hand on the man's elbow forcing him to the ground. The armlock looked like a classic police move and immediately forced the man to the floor.

"Let him go!" shouted an electronically enhanced voice.

Spartan knew when the voice of authority had arrived and this time it was in the shape of two armoured Military Policemen. They bore a striking similarity to the men he'd fought at the illegal fight and for a moment he was tempted to continue where he had left off. Then his brain kicked in and he recalled he'd only just got away with not going to prison. Spartan let the man go, leaving the two men on the floor. The third man lost control and was prancing about like a man high on drugs, probably trying to psyche himself up to fight him.

"Step back, hands in the air!" The second officer unclipped his shock maul, no doubt preparing himself for violence.

Spartan took a step back and raised his hands slightly, showing deference to the police, but not raising them too high to suggest guilt. The third man was having none of this and moved towards Spartan, presumably thinking he was vulnerable.

"Quit while you're still standing, pal!" he said with a snigger, adding the 'pal' for dramatic effect.

The man just couldn't see the situation for what it was and rushed forward. The first officer flipped out his maul and slammed it into the charging man's stomach. He went down hard, straight to the floor. Spartan just stood there, saying nothing. The second officer moved up to Spartan looking at him carefully, noting the marks and scars on his face.

"You looking for trouble here?"

"Not today," replied Spartan sarcastically.

The first officer laughed as he helped lift the men from the ground. "Get this out of your system, you've got plenty of time to sort this out, the trip to Prime is at least thirty-five long weeks. Lots of time to get acquainted." He then pushed them on.

The three men staggered along with Spartan following at a safe distance as the officers walked discreetly behind them. He was safe for now but as always he wasn't making friends.

As he reached the end of the corridor the crowd of people split into three smaller columns as they moved off to different parts of the shuttle. It was a big craft, much bigger than he'd expected. By his guess it could carry about two hundred people. He stepped inside noting almost all the seats had been taken. The three troublemakers were already sitting down and one was holding his nose, blood still dripping slowly from his exposure with the floor. The ginger-haired man smashed his hands together Spartan gave him a smile. It was futile but it made him feel better, for now anyway.

He spotted a seat a few rows back next to a Hispanic looking woman who was muttering to herself. Making his way across the craft he sat down and pulled the harness over his chest. Turning to the woman he held out his hand.

"Spartan, pleased to meet you."

She looked at him and then turned away, looking out of the window.

"Fair enough, you haven't hurt my feelings, I'm sure we'll get to meet again during basic." He looked back to the rest of the passengers.

In front of each line of seats were a series of pods hanging down with video displays. Each one was showing a commercial for the Confederate Marine Corps and no matter how hard he tried, Spartan couldn't contain himself and he let out a laugh. On the screen a single marine had just sheltered a child from a rain of bullets and then lifted the child to safety.

"Fucking Marine Corps propaganda!" shouted one of the men further inside the shuttle.

"Why are you here, Spartan, if you think this is so funny?" the woman next to him asked.

From the confined position in the shuttle he could only just make out her long, curly hair. She looked tiny compared to most of the hulking men there but Spartan knew from experience that a short woman was just as capable of knocking you down as a two-metre wrestler. If she knew what she was doing.

"It was this or prison."

"Prison? Did you make the right decision?"

He looked at her, confused by her question before spotting her wicked grin. Spartan laughed, appreciating a normal conversation that wasn't about to devolve into a fistfight.

"How about you then?"

"Foreclosure. They threatened to come in and take everything. The Judge ordered me on one tour to cover my debt or they will close my home down and take away my family."

"The asshole, looks like they nailed us both in the ass. What's your name?"

"Teresa," she replied, but added nothing else. She sat for a while before asking the question she was dying to know the answer to.

"So, did you do it?" she asked coyly.

"Well, I've done quite a bit," he answered with a grin. "What exactly did you have in mind?"

"Funny. You know what I meant. Why were you in court?"

Before he could answer the door slid shut with a sucking sound and the craft started to vibrate a little. The voice of the pilot came over the sound system.

"Captain Tyrol here. We are due for departure in thirty seconds. Please ensure your harnesses are fitted. We will be leaving the platform shortly and no harness means you'll drift and get hurt. All crew confirm status. Have a good flight."

Around the shuttle the crewmembers wandered about, checking the harnesses and hitting a few buttons near the seals on the doors. When they were satisfied they moved to their own seats and hit a sequence of controls. With a clunk the interior lighting switched off and was replaced by a dull glow from the transfer lights. There was a final sound and a hiss from manoeuvring thrusters. Spartan looked from his window and noticed they were drifting from the station dock. As the shuttle altered its course he could immediately feel the difference. Now they had broken free of their tether they were free floating in the zero gravity environment, it didn't appeal to Spartan at all.

"Crap!" he muttered as he grasped his harness to ensure he didn't drift out of his seat. The woman next to him laughed.

"So much for the mighty Spartan, I thought your scars meant you had seen action. Maybe you've just seen the wrong kind of action?" she laughed again.

"Nice." Spartan closed his eyes for a moment. With them shut he could concentrate on calming himself down and getting used to the feeling. It didn't take long and from what he had heard it was pretty common to feel a little nauseous in this situation. They had been in space for several minutes now and he didn't expect the journey would be that much longer. He gave it a few more seconds before opening his eyes. The Hispanic woman was staring right at him.

"You okay?"

"No problem," Spartan answered with a forced smile. "Now, what did you want to know?"

"What happened to you, Spartan?"

"I got screwed over just like you and they gave me a choice. No way was I going to prison, so here I am."

They sat in silence watching through the small windows as they approached the Santa Maria. It was clear how massive and old the ship was. The outer hull was marked with age and there were signs of damage and wear on many sections. They moved past the bow of the large ship and then alongside the habitation sections. These parts of the ship rotated but it wasn't where they were heading. Their speed reduced even further as they reached the loading area. A great hangar door was already open waiting for them. With great precision the pilot moved the shuttle in sideways and towards a platform. It took almost two minutes for them to be in the exact position before he lowered the craft. With a gentle clunk the magnetic seals locked it in place. From the wall a number of tubes like great tentacles pushed and headed towards the entry points on the shuttle. They slowly reached the body of the craft they linking with another clunk. Outside the main hangar door started to shut. Spartan gave one last look at the life he was leaving behind and then it was gone, the only light came from inside the shuttle.

"Welcome to the CCS Santa Maria. Please make sure you hold the rails as you leave. There is no gravity until you enter the first level of the habitation ring. Hope you enjoyed your short ride," said the pilot over the intercom system.

Almost as soon as the intercom switched off there was a loud gulping sound as the pressure normalised, then the door opened. Through the gaps the flexible access tubes led to the habitation section. The tube was wide enough for two people to walk abreast. Not that this was going to happen as they were all struggling to use the lowered hand rails in the zero gravity section of the ship. Spartan, now feeling comfortable in this environment let his legs drift and pulled himself along with his upper body. Looking back he noticed Teresa doing the same. As he expected she was much stronger than she looked. It took almost a full minute to reach the end of the tunnel and the bright light of the arrivals area.

Spartan paused as he reached the end, for a moment confused by what he saw ahead. As he entered the habitation ring he could see it rotating around him, people were all around the perimeter, though he was in the centre and still experiencing weightlessness. Ahead of him was a marine sergeant who was moving people down a series of ladders to the surface. He moved up to the marine who raised his hand to stop him.

"Wait. The ladder will take you down to the grav zone. You're gonna feel weird when you get hit by full on gravity again, so take it slow and wait if you feel nauseous."

Where he was waiting were four ladders, each rotating very slowly so that he could easily grab onto any of them.

He chose the one to his left and noted that he was already moving up slowly. Reaching out he grabbed the metal rung and swung his feet up onto the frame. At this point he was barely moving. Lowering himself down Spartan nodded and then started to work his way down the ladder. Although the section only rotated at about three complete revolutions a minute it was still moving at a considerable speed. Looking up he noticed Teresa was following close behind. He concentrated on the ladder and kept moving down until he finally reached the other section. He jumped down and was glad to feel the force of gravity pulling him to the outside of the vessel. He looked up to see the centre section where he had started seemed to be rotating though he knew it was actually him moving around it. He thought about it a little more, especially the idea that maybe he wasn't moving and maybe it was the centre section, then he gave up. Physics wasn't his forte and thinking about it for any longer he thought his head would explode.

There were over a hundred recruits now in this area and they were all busy looking around their new home. Though they were standing in what was essentially a big wheel, as they looked along the ship they could see the habitation section was just the other twenty metres or so that rotated around the main hull of the ship. It made sense, as the space in the centre would be a total waste if used as a zero gravity area to float around in. Teresa jumped down next to Spartan.

"That wasn't so bad now was it?"

"Yeah, bloody great!"

"Okay recruits, this is your last day as a civilian!"

Spartan turned to see a tall black man stood in his Marine Corps dress uniform. You have your berth numbers on this board and I suggest you get your gear unloaded. The time is set to Proxima Standard Time. That makes it fourteen hundred hours. We will re-assemble here in one hour for your introduction!"

Spartan approached the board and searched for his name. He noted he was in a section with three other men, none of them sounded familiar. Lifting his small backpack onto his shoulder he turned back to Teresa who was also reading the board.

"See you around, look after yourself."

Teresa smiled back, "Don't worry, I can take care of myself." She turned back to the screen.

Spartan moved off down the slightly curved corridor, reading the numbers on the berths as he went. Some of the doors were already open and he glimpsed a number of people putting their gear away. He reached his and noticed the door was shut. Pulling hard it swung open to reveal a small berth with two bunk beds one on each side and a small table in the middle. Against the far wall was a video terminal that had strong similarities with the screens back on the station. As he entered the room, it flickered and a three-dimensional face appeared.

"Welcome recruit. These are your quarters for the duration of your training. In this room you have adequate storage for your clothing and personal items. Communal showers and toilet facilities are between each eight berths. Video communications are available free of charge for all Marine Corps personnel but with the usual ten second security delay. Please exercise caution when using any outside communication devices. We are at war and information must always be guarded. Your briefing will take place in fifty-one minutes," said the voice before it went silent.

Another man entered the room, a tall black man with dark hair and a tattoo of a knife on his neck. Spartan scanned him quickly, instantly noting the way he moved and carried himself. Behind him were the final two men, a pair of Hispanics in their late twenties. The black man spoke first with a thick German accent.

"Marcus," he said, shaking Spartan's hands and then moved forward to one of the lower bunks. Spartan's gear was already on the top bunk to the right. The next two men entered, the first ignored everyone but the shorter one looked a little more agreeable.

"Jesus, and you?"

"Spartan."

"You Greek?"

"No," came the reply, in his usual sardonic manner.

"Oh, okay. Well, I guess I'm on the left."

With the four men now in the cabin, the artificial intelligence system reactivated and repeated the message Spartan had already listened to. He looked around, spotting the sprinklers system, fire extinguishers and fire axes. There was little that encouraged him as to the safety of the place. In fact, everything he had seen so far told him this vessel was far from the safest place he'd been in.

With a dull rumble through the massive vessel they could all feel the main engines on the ship start up. There was a slight rattle coming from one of the air vents. Jesus lifted himself up on the bunk bed and struck it with the palm of his hand, it changed nothing.

"Oh, man, that isn't going to annoy me is it?"

It wasn't clear whether Spartan was more irritated with Jesus or the vent but he quickly climbed up and smashed the bottom of his fist at the grate. It made a crunching sound and the rattle stopped instantly.

The German nodded his head in satisfaction grinning as he looked at the dent in the metalwork. "Yeah, I like your moves."

Spartan turned around with the room now quiet. "Me too."

The other Hispanic got up from the bunk bed and moved to Spartan. He was a good deal shorter but that didn't seem to bother him.

"Hey, man, I know you, yeah, Spartan," he said excitedly.

"I seriously doubt that."

"Yeah, you're that gladiator guy I saw on the news. You were fighting on one of the stations around Prometheus right? They said you killed a cop."

The German took a step back, staring warily at him. "Is that true, you a cop killer?"

"What does it matter, we're all here for the same reason, we were too stupid to do something better."

"Maybe, but I'd still like to know if I'm sharing with a cop killer."

"It was an accident, if it wasn't they'd have electrocuted my ass!"

"Accident my ass," said Jesus, as he jumped back onto his bunk.

"You looking to make an issue of it?" Spartan sounded more than a little annoyed.

"Just wondering, man, just wondering," smiled Jesus.

CHAPTER THREE

The Confederate Marine Corps serves as an amphibious force-in-readiness that is able to conduct operations both in and from space. As outlined in Title 32 of the Confederation Constitution and as originally introduced under the Confederation Security Act of 147b, it has three primary areas of responsibility:

These are the seizure or defence of ports, docks, and naval bases as well as land operations to support naval campaigns by the Centauri Confederate Navy fleet.

The development of tactics, techniques and equipment as used by amphibious landing forces.

Such other duties as the office of Command in Chief may direct.

History of the Marine Corps

The CCS Crusader was the newest and most powerful warship in the entire Fleet and for Lieutenant Erdeniz it was a dream posting. Of almost one hundred warships in the Fleet the Crusader was the place every crewmember wanted to serve on. Unlike the previous ships, the Crusader was the first battlecruiser to be built. The name had been used in the twentieth century and was a series of warships that were often of similar performance to battleships but armed with even more powerful weapons. In this respect she was similar but the emphasis was on speed. She carried much the same amount of weaponry as the larger battleships but had bigger engines and less substantial armour. It was all part of the Navy's new plans for faster ships that could respond to security incidents in the shortest time possible. With the increase in speed they would be able to protect the convoys from hijacked vessels' suicide attacks where problems could pop up anywhere in the System with no advance notice. Recent experience had shown the heavier, slower ships were easier to avoid and no armour could protect a vessel against a determined attack. The Crusader looked liked two upturned World War II battleships with their hulls fused together. There was no obvious top or bottom and there were a dozen rotating bands along the hull providing full and half gravity. With a crew complement of over two thousand, as well as over two hundred heavily equipped marines, the vessel was the ultimate form of force projection. Against the civilian transports and tenders it was a vessel of epic proportions in every way.

Lieutenant Erdeniz had graduated from the academy only a year before but was already stationed at one of the ship's massive weapon batteries. From his position, he commanded a ring of twenty-four weapons. They were divided into four batteries, each managed by a squad of six gunners, loaders and engineers. On this particular day, he was working with just one of the squads and their single weapon system.

He checked his screen as he worked on the configuration of a new weapons load out for his battery. Though the ship carried a variety of ordnance, the primary weapons were railguns. These were so large they could only be mounted in vessels such as this one and required massive nuclear generators to provide for their thirst for energy. He had modified enough ammunition for the entire battery and one test. He could get permission for no more.

The railgun weapon system was a fully electrical gun sending a conductive projectile along a pair of metal rails using the same principles as the homopolar motor. The system was first proposed in the early twentieth century but hit problems due to the massive power requirements. The railgun's batteries used two sliding contacts that permitted a large electric current to pass through the projectile. This current then interacted with the strong magnetic fields generated by the rails accelerating the projectile to an incredibly fast speed. Anything hit by the speeding ammunition would be torn apart by the sheer kinetic energy. Lieutenant Erdeniz had proposed a variant on one normal solid shot used to provide a weapon with similar characteristics to the canister rounds used by wooden sailing ships.

Today was a very special day, as he would test his creation in front of a panel of senior officers from the crew of the ship. He wore his dress uniform and it was a decision he was already regretting. He might be a lieutenant but in front of these officers he felt like a child. He had been proposing this new weapon system for three months and it had taken weeks of permission forms and testing before they would even consider his suggestion. If he could make it work he could expect an immediate promotion. Of course, if for any reason the system didn't work he could be looking at all manner of problems, not least a black mark on his record that might prove impossible to remove. There was also the very tiny possibility that if the system failed it could cause expensive damage to the weapon systems. That would immediately put an end to his chances of promotion in the future.

Lieutenant Erdeniz stood up stiffly as more of the officers entered the gunnery section. His crew stood smartly to attention, as did he. The room was cramped and although the men did a good job at keeping the place clear and smart it still looked like an old steam ship's engine room. It was hardly a place befitting these high rankers.

General Rivers approached and shook his hand. He was tall and had the reputation of a man with years of active service and combat to go with it. He had been busy in the last few years fighting the many pirate groups popping up and had achieved some important victories.

"I've read your recommendations and I like your work. I know there are many who say the weapon is pointless and that it saps energy from the main projectile, but I'm convinced it could have a use." He then stepped back.

Another officer, Captain Jackson, was less than impressed and stood nearby but said nothing. He'd been arguing for the use of high explosive based weapons and if Lieutenant Erdeniz's system didn't work, they might well look to him.

"Please proceed," said the General.

Lieutenant Erdeniz moved his hands in front of the display and a three dimensional model of the battlecruiser appeared. He moved to the side and explained the situation.

"In this simulated engagement we see a vessel is approaching, it is actually approximately five thousand metres away but it could quite easily be five hundred. The vessel is based upon collisions we have faced recently," he said as calmly as possible.

The group watching seemed unexcited at the task so far, so Erdeniz turned to his crew to get it moving more quickly.

"What is the estimated damage of impact from that vessel?"

"Based on its current velocity we are looking at a forty percent loss of Section B with around twenty decks destroyed. This will cut the power to all batteries forward of Section C," replied Ensign Harris.

Erdeniz returned to the screen as the model showed the ship crashing into the side of the warship and causing catastrophic damage.

"As we know, the armour of this vessel is thinner than the battleships, especially in these zones. At this speed we are looking at the very best, a heavily damaged barely operational warship and at worse a crippled vessel."

"Okay, son, we appreciate the problem, can you show us your weapon now?" said the agitated Captain.

Erdeniz nodded and proceeded to start the weapon sequence.

"I will fire two shots from this main gun. The first is our standard heavy shot and the second my canister variant. If you will all watch this screen, I have sent out two camera drones to monitor the demonstration."

On cue the screen flickered and multiple views appeared on the wall that gave the impression of a large window they could all see out. The illusion also allowed him to make the approaching vessel appear much closer that it really was.

"The first shot, our standard eight hundred millimetre

armour piercing round is loaded and ready." There was a clunk as the seals were shut.

Erdeniz flipped a hatch open to reveal a series of buttons and a red glowing button the centre.

"Gun ready?"

"Aye," replied his crew.

"Fire!" He hit the launch button.

There was a loud buzz through the floor of the room as the weapon system accelerated the massive man-sized round along the rails and out of the gun port fitted on the side of the hull. The external camera couldn't capture the shell itself as it moved at such an incredibly high speed. From the gun port however a plume of superheated plasma gushed out, much like the gun port on a medieval warship.

The second camera showed the almost immediate impact on the approaching ship. It struck the outer hull and tore a metre-wide gash before blasting through the vessel and out through the other side.

"As you can see, the shell is easily capable of penetrating any current armour types. The big problem is that it passes clean through the ship."

"So why not just fit a proximity fuse on the shell and explode it inside the target?" asked one of the officers.

"A good point and one we have already tried. The issues are with the shells themselves. At these massive speeds we have to use electronics to get the timing right. By the time the shell hits the hull and triggers the explosive it has already passed through the ship. Electronics can calculate the distance but all military vessels are fitted with electronic jamming equipment that can detonate the shell before it gets anywhere near the ship. My weapon system uses a simple preset mechanical timer that causes the shell to split a given distance from the ship, the default being when it reaches the distance of one hundred metres. Once activated the shells breaks into seventy two separate shards, each one travelling just a few degrees off the original line of fire."

"Okay, I'm sold on the idea, let's see it in action!" The General said with a half-hearted grin.

Erdeniz turned back to his crew, about to check the weapon was loaded when the door opened and in walked Admiral Jarvis. She was in her early forties and rarely seen anywhere near the gun decks of the ship. As Admiral of the Fleet, she had her flag on this vessel but she had an entire fleet to manage. It was an unprecedented honour to have her here. As she entered, the rest of the officers stood to attention. The Admiral moved directly to Erdeniz ignoring everyone else.

"Your report makes interesting reading, Lieutenant, is your experiment ready?"

"Yes, Admiral, we were about to fire a test round."

"Excellent, continue." She remained in the same place, right in the centre of the room.

Erdeniz turned to his gun crew who by now were looking even more nervous than he was. He doubted they had ever seen so many officers in one place.

"Canister round loaded and ready?"

"Aye!" came the reply once again.

"Fire!"

The same buzz as before and as far as the officers could tell the system also worked exactly the same until they spotted the damage on the approaching ship. All along the side were a vast number of craters and chunks of metal in a cloud of dust and debris. The crew stood back, watching the screens as the debris moved away to reveal the targeted vessel.

Erdeniz prayed and prayed, hoping that his efforts would be vindicated. It had cost a lot of manpower and materials to get this test. He looked at the centre of the screen as the automated camera tried to focus on the many targets, then it cleared.

"Holy shit!" said the General.

The debris had shifted far enough now that the approaching ship could be seen in great detail. First, and foremost, the entire middle section was torn to shreds. A great hole, easily five times the size of the original shell impact had cut through and torn the backbone of the ship apart. Additional small holes were scattered across multiple sections leaving many parts of the vessel either completely blasted off or hanging down in chunks.

They all burst into applause, much to the relief of Erdeniz who watched with a mixture of pride and happiness. It had taken a lot of effort but finally the Canister Round was ready for experimental use aboard the newest ship in the Fleet. Admiral Jarvis moved until she stood directly in front of him.

"Good job, Lieutenant, I had a feeling this was going to work. According to your research paper you took many ideas from the British, specifically Admiral Nelson?"

"Yes, Admiral."

"When I was a cadet I was assigned the Battle of the Nile as my research project. Nelson showed what daring and cunning could do, even when outnumbered. He liked to get close and I can see why you thought of this for our vessels. We have a major weakness and I think you might be on the way to fixing at least a part of it. How soon can you modify our weapons and will the ammunition types be interchangeable?"

"The software is simple to change. I can do that from here. The ammunition needs a slight modification. With the facilities here I can organises stocks of rounds in about three days. Certainly enough for a few volleys."

"Excellent. I want this gunnery crew and all their guns to have access to this ammunition. We will trial it over the next few weeks. If it goes as well as your tests I think we'll be seeing the Sanlav Round being deployed through the Fleet."

He saluted as the Admiral left the room. As she left Erdeniz allowed himself to bask in the glow of success at the success of his weapon test and even better, the fact that the Admiral knew his name. Perhaps things were starting to look up for Lieutenant Sanlav Erdeniz.

* * *

Onboard the CCS Santa Maria it was the third week of training and contrary to his expectations, Spartan was actually starting to enjoy himself. In the first two weeks he had already gone through the gruelling ordeal of Gym, Mathematics and English Assessment as well as the start of basic drill and training.

In the first days they had split the recruits up into squads and platoons. He was getting to know his other platoon companions quite well. They didn't all get on of course, there was the odd rumour about why he was there, but on the whole there was a certain level of respect for each other.

As expected he did much better on the physical than the mental side but it wasn't as bad as he thought. Either that or perhaps the competition wasn't as far advanced in the learning stakes as he thought they might be. He easily passed the initial assessment for combat training which meant it was more likely to lead to a frontline posting. He much preferred that to the other posts on offer such as intelligence, command or engineering. The last thing he wanted was to be stuck in an office dying of boredom while the rest of the recruits got to experience the full life as a marine. If he had to spend ten years doing this then he was going to give it his damned best.

He stood in line along with the rest of his training platoon. There were thirty-six of them and now technically classed as privates though the drill instructor called them all 'recruits'. The term marine was only applied after completing training and being accepted by the Sergeant as fit and able. The title had to be earned, at least that's what he kept saying. The group was diverse in every way. There were blacks, Hispanics, men and women. The age range was also surprising, from early twenties right up to some in their forties.

The training hall was in yet another part of the full gravity section of the ship and to all intents and purposes looked like any other training hall, apart from a slight curve in the floor. Along the walls was a selection of training tools, weights, equipment and even firearms, though they were locked in cabinets. There were no windows and the light was bright, really bright. As they stood to attention their Drill Sergeant approached, he matched almost every stereotype he'd ever heard of. The man was clean-shaven, a good two metres tall with the trim and muscled body of a man who took his job very seriously. He strolled in front before stopping in the centre and turning to face them.

"Okay, ladies, today is close quarter combat day. I am going to instruct you in the sophisticated art of using every part of the body as a lethal fighting machine. In the Marine Corps it is every marine's duty to be able to defend himself whether you are armed or not." He looked directly at Spartan.

Without saying anything he moved up to him and walked back and forth, examining him in detail. Like the rest of the recruits, Spartan wore a pair of shorts and a t-shirt. His body was unlike any of the others there. Some were bigger and others undoubtedly stronger but none had the mixture of muscles, fitness and scars that he carried.

"What's your name, son?"

"Spartan!" he answered quickly.

"In the CMC it is polite to refer to me as Sergeant, Sir or Drill Instructor! Now, shall we try that again?"

"Spartan, Sir!"

"Oh, yeah, I've heard of you. You're some kind of gladiator, bet the girlies get excited when they see you." He sneered and then shouted.

"Recruit Spartan, three steps forward!"

Spartan, without hesitating stepped ahead and the instructor walked around him.

"This is an example of a marine's body. He looks strong, is fit and has the marks of a man who has seen action. There is one thing that makes him different though. He works alone, he is not part of a team and he fights for pleasure or money! He might look like a marine but a marine his is not!"

"You, you, you and you! Forward!" He pointed at the four weakest members of the platoon.

The two women and two men moved ahead, each looking nervous as they stood unprotected at the front.

"You four are pathetic, look at you!" The Sergeant shouted at them.

A giggle came from the back of the group where Jesus was pushed into the back row.

"Stop! Who did that?" The instructor marched up the line but nobody responded.

"So help me, God, you have five seconds or the entire platoon will suffer. Who did that?"

"I did," came a sheepish response from Jesus.

"I did?"

"I did, Sergeant," said Jesus as he remembered the correct form.

The instructor grinned to himself for a moment before continuing. "You snivelling piece of shit. You think learning to be a marine is funny? When you are face down in the dirt fighting those Zealot bastards are you gonna be laughing then? Let me tell you, son. In my last tour I saw smart asses like you get themselves cut in half by improvised explosives. And there was nothing anybody could do to help them! One marine is an asset and an entire platoon is unstoppable. If you treat them with contempt you treat the Corps with contempt, now get your ass to the front!"

Jesus moved quickly and joined the other four recruits. Spartan was still stood alone and said nothing though he wasn't convinced he was going to like what came next. The drill instructor rubbed his hands together with glee.

"Now, let's find out what you have. You are going to learn an important lesson today and if you're smart you'll stay out of the medical bay. You're going to show the platoon how to bring a man like Spartan down!"

Jesus looked at Spartan and back at the drill instructor. "What the fuck?"

The instructor moved right in front of him, his look of humour having vanished.

"What's the matter, pretty boy? You worried the big man will treat you like his bitch? What if you five are unarmed and face an enemy? You gonna cry to momma or are you going to stand up and be a marine? There are five of you. Now, get in there and show us you have what it takes!"

Spartan knew it was coming and turned to face the five of them. He was by far the biggest, but they still had the advantage of numbers, and who knows what skills or training they might have.

"I'm waiting!" barked the instructor.

Jesus, obviously feeling the pressure rushed forward as the other four looked on in a mixture of fear and confusion. The distance was only five metres but by the time he was close enough to reach Spartan, it was clear to everybody how it was going to go. Jesus ran right up to the man, presumably expecting to throw him to the floor. As he reached grabbing distance, Spartan lowered his body slamming his shoulder into the man's stomach. The impact and speed of the strike forced the air out of his lungs nearly knocking him out. With him doubled over, Spartan brought his left elbow down to strike on his back and it was over. Jesus lay face down on the floor and Spartan stood up to face the other four. The drill instructor stood smiling as he watched.

"Bravo, bravo. An excellent lesson in what not to do." He turned to the four that were left. "Well?" he asked sarcastically.

Three of the group inched forward but the fourth, the younger of the women, stayed back not sure as to what she should be doing. The tallest of the three was a well-built middle-aged man and he made the first move. He stepped closer though unlike Jesus he adopted a traditional boxing stance. His left foot was forward and both his hands held up to protect his face.

Spartan moved towards him, quickly closing the distance until they were within easy punching range. Unlike his opponent, Spartan had his hands much lower and he looked relaxed, almost unready. The black haired woman, with the younger man, moved to his flanks. They obviously felt more confident with the more experienced man taking the centre position. Spartan noted the way the man moved, he'd had a decent amount of boxing training at the very least. Spartan threw a couple of light jabs to get his hands up and then took two strong steps to the right to face the younger man. His face turned to stone as Spartan smashed his fist hard into the man's jaw and sent him tumbling to the ground. Spartan turned quickly back to face the boxer when the dark haired woman moved nearer. She was trying to do something though it seemed she didn't know what.

The boxer moved in and caught him with a punch to the arm, then moved in to try for a hit to his head. Luckily, Spartan's reactions were fast enough that he was able to avoid the second strike but not fast enough to stop the woman jumping on him. She hung onto his shoulder and her weight pushed him off balance.

Spotting the turn of the tide the woman hit him repeatedly on the side of the head with her hands as the second woman ran over to join in, trying to hold him down. He struggled and fought but between the two of them and the big guy he couldn't move. The man lowered himself down and punched him twice in the stomach, instantly making him gasp for air. It wasn't enough though, Spartan had been in much worse positions. Sensing his foes thought they had the upper hand he grabbed the first woman with his legs in a strong pincer like movement. She cried out as he squeezed her, following up with a head-butt to the boxer.

He stumbled backwards but managed to stand up straight. The woman he'd locked with his legs was easily dealt with as he kicked her in the side, rolling her away from him. Blood ran down from the boxer's nose, dripping from his lip to the floor. With this brief respite Spartan was able to strike the second woman with the base of his fist and then release himself from his position on the ground. She tumbled backwards, clutching her left arm that was at the very least dislocated. Jesus was still lying on the floor as the kicked woman lay groaning.

"Enough!" The Drill Instructor shouted.

Spartan relaxed a little as he lifted his body up straight and waited for whatever was coming next. With a couple of hand gestures three medics ran in, each checking on the injured recruits though none bothered to head for Spartan, not that he was that concerned, he barely even considered that a fight.

"As you can see, even a man like Spartan can be brought down by the co-ordinated use of appropriate numbers. A man called Lanchester created a set of laws for calculating the relative strengths of a predator and prey pair. These laws have been used ever since to help calculate the combat effectiveness of units when placed together and we can confirm their accuracy from real world testing. Place two men of the same skills together and the fight can go either way. Place two on one side and how often does the paired team win? Twice as likely as before or more?"

The room was silent as the recruits listened though not really knowing what to say. The Drill Sergeant walked around them, pretending to listen for answers.

"It is simple, very simple. The combat power of a unit increases by a much, much higher factor as the numbers increase. Two against one can easily expect to win four out of five matches, often more. This is because when working together you massively increase your individual effectiveness!"

Walking along the line, he stopped at Spartan.

"Even more importantly it means that two average fighters can take on and beat a better one. That is why you work together and do not do what Jesus did here and run out on your own. There is no glory in letting down your squad. You get me?"

"We get you, Sergeant!" came the chorus from the recruits.

"Now, while these newbies get some basic medical attention I am going to introduce you to the fine art of combat. You will learn to breathe, move, strike, punch, kick, block, throw and stab. By the time I have finished with you, you will be able to fight no matter what your condition is or what weapons you have. You are a marine at all times and you are expected to fight like a marine at all times!"

He moved over to the wall and gave a signal. The room darkened and a series of images popped up. Each image showed various fighting moves though some looked antiquated and from unfamiliar cultures.

"Now, what we have here is a selection of images from fighting manuals going right back to the middle ages. Note how they are standing, how they move and throw their opponents. In the last few thousand years the human body has changed in almost no discernable fashion. What was true for a Roman soldier at the time of Christ is true today. You can break an arm, sever an artery or crush a windpipe. This is true for all of humanity and it will remain so for a good time to come. These images are from the manuals of those before us who knew EXACTLY what they were doing." He paused, looking at a weedy looking man.

"You, recruit snot brain, here now!"

The man looked around before realising he was being pointed at. He then rushed to the front and stood at attention in front of the Sergeant. The instructor reached down and pulled out a standard issue marine's knife and placed it in his hand.

"Stab me, son, right in the heart!"

The man was obviously terrified of either messing it up or hurting the instructor, so simply stood there, and doing nothing.

"Do it, boy or I'll try it on you!"

With a scream the man pushed it forward aiming for

the centre of the man's chest. With a simple move the Sergeant grabbed the man's arm pulling him past before he snapped it up behind him. The man dropped to his knees whimpering.

"Now, look at the image on the right, it is from a late twentieth century riot police training film. Notice how the officer is restraining the man. That's right, ladies, he's using the same damned technique."

"Back in line, boy!" He looked around he group.

"You!" he said as he spotted the big German.

The man moved to the front without the fear and hesitation the younger man had. The Sergeant passed him the knife.

"Stab me here, down through my collar and in….." he was unable to finish his sentence as the man was already moving to strike him.

The Sergeant incredibly lifted his right arm, struck the inside of the German and brushed the knife hand away from him. Then he brought up his left, slamming the back of his fist into the German's jaw. It sent a cloud of blood from his mouth and into the faces of the recruits stood behind him. The German staggered back as he lifted his hand to his mouth. Another medic ran over and placed a pack on his face before moving to the back.

"Image four, this one is from a medieval fighting manual by a man called Talhoffer. Note the way he has displaced the knife attack and then struck his attacker in the jaw. These people knew their business. A punch, stab or strike is the same the galaxy over and you have months to perfect your skills. Now look at the rest of these images. In the fourteenth century the German fencing masters taught a complete system for a warrior to be able to fight in all circumstances." As he spoke a sequence of images appeared from the manual.

"Each man would learn how to fight without a weapon. He needed to know how to stop a knife attack, a very common weapon that all would carry, how to throw a man down or how to break limbs. He was then taught to use a sword, a two handed sword, a long knife like a machete, spears, pole arms. I think you get the picture." As he finished the lights came back up.

One of the marines approached from one of the storerooms with what looked like a toolbox and placed it on the ground. The drill sergeant reached inside and pulled out a large fighting knife.

"This here is the M11 Bayonet. As well as doubling for a bayonet on your rifle it is also designed to be one hell of a fighting knife." He flipped the knife around so everybody could see the tip.

"It features a sharp, heat hardened point that helps penetrate the body armour that many of our adversaries will be wearing. The serrations near the handle help improve its function as a utility knife, so you will want to look after this fine piece of equipment. The M11

Bayonet is made from high carbon steel and is capable of functioning without breakage in operating temperatures in excess of -25 to 135 degrees farenheit. This means we can use this weapon in all environments where we expect trouble, and then some."

Leaning down he pulled open the lid to reveal scores of the blades, each neatly packed away inside their sheath. He pulled another out and waved it at the recruits.

"This is your first piece of gear and you will respect it. Wherever you go and whatever duties you are carrying out you will always carry this weapon with you." He stood up. "Now, each of you take your knife and get back in line."

It took less than a minute for them all to take their knives before they were back in position. The Drill Sergeant waited for a short while before continuing.

A group of marines walked in, pulling behind them a set of six life-size dummies attached to stands. The dummies were perfect doubles for humans apart from lacking any discernable clothes. They positioned them in a neat line facing the recruits and then left the room. The Drill Sergeant walked along the line of dummies, looking at the various nicks and marks from where they had been used scores of times before. In a move that surprised the recruits he flipped his own knife from his sheath and stabbed the first in the collar, then the same on the other side and then slashes across the throat before returning the blade. He stopped, tucked in his shirt and then turned to the recruits.

"You might think this weapon is a waste of time in this decade of advanced armours, state of the art rifles and space travel. But let me tell you, a knife can be used silently and discreetly. It can be hidden if you are captured and may be used for hundreds of non-combat related roles. If you can kill with a knife you can kill with a rifle!" He took a few more steps before halting and continuing his speech.

"Today we are going to start with knife training. First, you will learn how to stab and cut at the important parts of the body. When you are ready, I will then teach you the defences to all these attacks. Are you ready?" he shouted.

"Yes, Drill Sergeant!" the group stood to attention and shouted in chorus.

CHAPTER FOUR

The exact origins of the Zealots are still uncertain and their appearance on Proxima Prime has never been explained. Many colonists brought their sects and religions to their new homes but this cult quickly spread through the workers in the mining community. From there it spread like wildfire in the impoverished sections of society until they exploded into violence.

The demands of the Zealots have always been simple. They are a brotherhood that provides moral and physical guidance, their way is the one true way and it is their duty to help others come to that realisation.

It took less than six months for the cult to build their first bomb and to claim their first victim. After the Ontario incident, it took just weeks for similar attacks to spread. The message is clear. The Zealots will accept full conversion, nothing less.

In the years and months that followed the terms insurgents, terrorists and Zealots came to mean the same thing.

A Brief History of the Zealots

This was no fancy yacht or military ship, the TS Younara Glory was one of the largest transports in the shipping industry. A single shipment from this vessel promised massive profits for the company and this was no doubt why their competitors were all racing to produce vessels of a similar capacity.

Since her launch four years ago, she spent her time ploughing the trade routes of Proxima to deliver her cargo of freshly mined minerals and materials. The ship was nearly two kilometres long and almost entirely automated. In theory the entire operation could be conducted without human intervention of any kind. In fact, there were many reasons why taking humans out of the loop entirely would be advantageous. Nonetheless, with such a high price tag on both the vessel and the cargo it was a requirement for any shipping insurance that a small crew was present at all times. If nothing else, should the ship end up crashing into a station there would be humans to blame, assuming any lived of course. A computer or mechanical failure could cause all kinds of problems in deep space and a crew could provide options a computer system might overlook. For those who might be aesthetically minded, she would appear to be an ugly ship. The basic shape was like a giant bell with the rear of the ship massively larger than the front. The great mess of metal expanded in all directions to provide for the numerous storage areas for the raw materials. All around the outer rim additional gantry sections provided mountings for cranes and tooling to use in the movement and extraction of storage containers. Towards the front were three lifeboats, all accessible from the crew's habitation module, each able to carry all the members of the crew.

At the rear were a dozen massive engines, each running continually to provide the thrust for the return voyage. The ion thruster was a very common form of advanced electric propulsion used for spacecraft propulsion. The basic principle was that they created thrust by accelerating ions. The electrostatic ion thrusters used Coulomb force and worked by accelerating the ions in the direction of the electric field. The ion engines were commonly used on this type of vessel. They were extremely efficient and could provide continuous, reliable thrust over years and years. The only downside to these engines was that they took weeks to be able to start pushing such a mass through space. This was why the Younara Glory followed a continuous elliptical orbit that was beautifully timed to allow her to pass both collection and delivery points on her voyage without stopping. This was a major feat of navigation as it required the vessel to match the orbital stations positions long enough to move materials before moving on. For the time when the ship needed extra power at short notice the manoeuvring engines were available. These huge power plants were even more substantial than the ion drives. But they had couldn't provide the continuous power of the ion engines and would burn up all their fuel in less than a week compared to the forty year power plant lifespan of the ion system. This long, monotonous journey was why so much automation was required, and why the crews were able to command such high salaries.

Down the side of the vessel was a thick double white stripe, the famous symbol of the Trans Shipping Corporation. At the front was a large rotating wheel, much like a Catherine Wheel. It added a peculiar look to the already angry looking vessel. This section provided all the facilities the small number of crew would need for a twelve-month assignment.

She had been in transit now for two months and was coming to the end of her voyage. The twin stars of Alpha Centauri burned brightly but at this distance the refinery and space dock were impossible to see. It would take another week for them to reach Proxima Prime, the largest colonised planet in the Proxima Centauri System though they were not visiting the planet. The drop off point was the Titan Naval Station, a massive complex that had been built into Kronus, one of the planet's smaller moons. At some point in the past it looked like any other rocky satellite, but decades of engineering, terraforming and heavy work had turned it into a habitable and busy colony in its own right. From space, the surface of the moon looked completely man-made.

It was one of the most important ports and transport hubs in the entire System with a combined civilian and military population in excess of two million people. All major freight and passenger transport vessels used the Station when on long journeys or transporting major cargos. Due to its orbit around Proxima Prime it also served as the perfect jumping off point for anybody looking to leave the planet. At any point in the day there were at least a dozen shuttles moving between the planet's surface and the moon base. With around one quarter of normal gravity it was much easier to build and maintain craft, as opposed to trying to get them through the planet's atmosphere and all the problems that entailed. The Titan Naval Station was also home to the Proxima Squadron, the elite and most well trained part of the Confederation Fleet and responsible for the defence of this area against terrorism, piracy and hijacking. The Proxima Squadron was based around two battleships and over a dozens frigates and transports. It had the numbers and firepower to settle any problems or disputes that might arise.

The huge transport was a tiny spec in comparison to her destination docking point. At the front of the vessel the crew module contained several small rooms including a canteen and kitchen, fitness room and navigation centre. At first glance, it might appear over generous but after the first week it was well known how irritable and troublesome a crew could be.

The crew were sitting around a small round table in the mess. It was dark and cramped but there was little space available to them that wasn't packed full of cargo. On the centre of the table was the usual collection of artefacts signalling the closing stages of a card game where the players had taken things possibly a little too far. The large pile by far was the luxury food items, closely followed by coins and then a spurious pile of oddities that must have been added as the desperation stakes climbed.

Captain Thomas checked his cards, it wasn't going well for him. The last card had put him in the unenviable position of having to withdraw and he was less than impressed. Dropping his cards onto the table he looked at Casey, his adversary rubbed his head.

"I fold!"

Casey smiled and made to move forward to grab his winnings when he was interrupted by the emergency alarm. As the sound reverberated around the room, the lighting cut to emergency mode. As with most vessels of this kind the low level red lighting used minimal power and didn't interfere with night vision as much as the normal harsh lights.

"What the hell?" said Jackson, as he looked around.

"Shit, that is a bad sound, I know that!" Traci replied with a slight hint of sarcasm.

Captain Thomas, the older but experienced officer was the first to stand and made his way out of the door. He ignored the rest of the crew as they tried to catch up. This was his first emergency on this ship and being as they travelled along a clear and safe transit route it must be serious if the computer system was reporting it. As they made their way through the corridors, the ship's built-in computer system was activated.

"Proximity Alert! Proximity Alert!" The message repeated as they entered the bridge area.

The screens were all live and Captain Thomas jumped into his chair, waving his hands as he moved through the pages of data. He stopped on one that displayed a number of small objects.

"I'm getting readings on twelve small vessels, they look like life pods to me," said Jackson.

Wilkinson arrived and checked his screens. "I have life readings in all of them, it looks like two people per pod."

"Two per pod? That is strange, can you confirm that?"

He continued looking through the screens of data on the various displays, checking on the communication and navigation logs for signs of trouble. One entry got his attention, it was concerned with a missing tug. Bringing up the story it appeared a vessel had disappeared in this same area two weeks ago. The crew compliment was forty-two including several passengers.

"Sir, I've got a report here on a missing vessel, it could be them, if so they've been out here for some time."

"We don't really have the space for them but we can't leave them out there. Wilkinson, get down to the airlock and help them in. Mathews, get the bots out and bring in the pods." The Captain ordered.

The only woman in the crew, Traci, was the medical officer and doubled as the security chief. She moved to the weapons' locker on the wall with a look of someone who always expected the worst.

"Traci, get down to the airlocks and help Wilkinson, they may have casualties amongst them."

She flipped open the cupboard and removed a firearm. It was a civilian issue C14 carbine fitted with ultra low velocity rounds designed for use against un-armoured targets. Anything more could risk a breach in the habitation section and a breach quite simply meant death. The weapon was quite rounded, partially for aesthetics and to ensure it didn't catch or damage anything important when being used in space. Military grade firearms were only available on military vessels and even then usually issued prior to action, due to the inherent danger of weapons in space. She moved into the side corridor that led down to the main access section and airlocks. The room was hexagonal shaped and equipped with four airlock seals. As she reached the computer terminal between two of the seals she felt the clunk of the first of the pods pushing against the sprung section.

"Weird?" She checked all the valves prior to starting the airlock sequence. The changes in pressure could be fatal and must be normalised safely prior to anybody coming aboard.

Wilkinson was already lowering a set of doors that operated as beds or seats as he checked the status of the pods on his hand-held computer.

"I don't get it, these readings show they are over a minute away, the bots have only just started."

A loud noise hit the side of the section and then a dull throbbing sound started pounding on the furthest airlock door. It sounded like a badly aligned motor or a wheel on an automobile that wasn't properly balanced.

"Get back!" Traci shouted as she moved away from the airlock and back into the corridor. She pulled the carbine from her should and held it in front of her. It seemed like any other weapon apart from having a much wider muzzle and a magazine that held six shots. The wider muzzle was due to the large, low velocity rubberised slug the weapon fired. She reached out to a panel on the wall revealing an intercom system and hit the button.

"Captain, what's going on out there? We've got something at the airlock already. Captain, please respond, we've got a situation down here!"

There was no response and they stood in silence,

watching the airlock with a mixture of fear and curiosity. Traci hit her fist on the seal button and an additional seal came down in the middle of the corridor, cutting them off from the airlock section in case of a breach.

Then the airlock seals blew. The pressure change was not as great as she would have expected but it was enough to make her stumble as the section shook from the movement. The entire section was temporarily flooded with a mist that blocked visibility up to the sealed area.

"You okay?" Wilkinson asked her as he held onto the wall.

"Yeah, what was that?" She tried to check the screen to her right. The display was showing garbage, as though the software had crashed or been jammed. Another series of blasts shook the habitation part of the ship and they were forced to hang onto the sides of the shaft. Casey's head appeared at the far end as he shouted down.

"We've got breaches in the loading bay, Jackson is checking it out. You okay down there, Traci?"

"Yeah, I've closed the shaft seal for now, looks like one of them must have hit an airlock mount, the pressure just shifted, nothing too serious though."

There was another clunking sound followed by noises at the bridge. Casey turned and disappeared from view. There was a shout then nothing.

"Come on! The bridge!" Traci shouted as she rushed along the shaft to the Captain and Casey. As she rounded the corner she came face to face with Casey. His hands were low and holding his stomach. A dark red patch spread across his clothes and then she noticed the tip of a weapon extending from his flesh. With a sliding sound it disappeared and he slumped forward. Wilkinson jumped ahead, catching the dying man as he fell.

Traci lifted her carbine to her shoulder and quickly scanned the room. Just beyond where Casey had been standing was a man in a long flowing robe. She could just make out sections of scale-like armour, though they were so thin it looked more like a patterned tunic. The man's head was covered in the traditional hood of the Zealots.

Without pausing, she fired a round directly at the man. He was taken by surprise and it hit him squarely in the chest, kicking him back almost a metre before he managed to straighten himself up. He looked down at the hole the bullet had made on his robe and with a snort ripped it off, exposing his body armour in all its finery.

Though Traci had never met one, she had heard of the Zealot infiltration teams from the security briefs they held every six months. These men were notorious for their attacks on civilian transports but never this far from the planet. He didn't appear to be carrying any firearms though he did have a short, savage looking blade attached to his right arm. It was serrated along its back edge and reminded her of something from a pirate adventure in books she had read as a child.

"He's dead." Wilkinson stood up and grabbed an emergency axe from the wall. "This bastard is mine!"

The axe was light and balanced for single hand use. As he swung the weapon the Zealot leapt to the side, parrying it with a single neat move and then counter slashed into Wilkinson. The technique was perfect and left a great wound from his thigh to his armpit. Wilkinson cried out in pain before collapsing near the Captain's chair. It was then that Traci spotted the Captain's body slumped in the chair. He had multiple wounds on his torso.

The man turned to Traci, a foul sneer forming on his lip.

"What is a woman doing working as crew on a commercial vessel? Do you not have a family to attend?" he said angrily.

"A family? What the fuck!" She cried out and then emptied the rest of the carbine's ammunition into the man. Though they were obviously incapable of penetrating his armour they could certainly incapacitate anyone they struck in the face.

The shots were well aimed and the first struck him in the cheek causing a superficial but bloody wound. The subsequent rounds hammered around his head and shoulder but he managed to twist bringing his left arm up to absorb the impact. As the kinetic energy blasted him backwards she rushed in, the carbine held high and with the butt facing forward. As she moved ahead she heard screams coming from below, presumably the loading bay. She reached the wounded man who moved to get up from the floor. Her combat training kicked in and she didn't give him the chance to get up as she slid down and slammed the carbine into his face. There was a sickening crunch as the weapon crushed his nose and sent blood spraying into her eyes. It wasn't enough though and she struck again and again until he moved no more.

Traci rolled away from the bloody body of the man and looked back towards the badly injured Wilkinson who was still crying in pain from his wicked wound.

"Wilks, hey, Wilks!"

He was in too much pain to notice her shouts and continued to roll back and forth in pain. Traci moved along the slippery floor until she reached the hurt man. As she bent down to help she spotted two figures stood in the room staring at her. They were dressed the same as the first man but didn't wear cloaks. Each carried the same vicious looking blades in their hands and both had seen their dead brethren in the corner of the room. Traci stood up, still holding the now damaged carbine and lifted it up, ready to fight.

The man to the left reached down to a pouch on his right leg and pulled out a heavily modified pistol of unknown manufacture. Like the rest of their equipment it had a blade fitted to the muzzle with ridges running along the barrel. Traci knew it was over and rather than wait she rushed. The men were taken by surprise and her speed truly was impressive. Her first three steps brought her almost within striking range before the man fired. The first bullet struck her in the shoulder and then more spread across her chest. She collapsed just in front of the men, blood pouring from her wounds. She tried to get up but it was no good, she was finished. As she slumped down she heard the intercom crackle, it was Jackson.

"I'm hurt, some guy just broke in and tried to space me. I need medical attention down here. Hurry, please hurry!"

Traci tried to speak and then the darkness crept over her eyes and her pain vanished.

* * *

They had just finished a gruelling three-hour mixed martial arts session and Spartan was exhausted. He stood in the shower, both hands hanging low as the water poured out and down his back. He'd not been expecting showers but the water reclamation and recycling system on the ship seemed pretty efficient, certainly better than no showers. Around him the rest of his platoon were doing the same. At first it had been odd, but after weeks of training he and the rest of the mixed unit were too tired to really care anymore. As far as he could see a line of naked men and woman simply used the opportunity to relax. As he washed away the sweat and grime he spotted the Hispanic woman he'd first met when leaving the station.

"Teresa," he muttered to himself as he remembered her name.

After just a few seconds he went across the shower block, moving the odd person who always seemed to get in the way. As he approached he felt a pang of embarrassment as he saw her naked. Her skin was dark and the water ran down her making her body glisten. Her black hair seemed longer in the shower, it ran down to her shoulders and for some reason all Spartan could think about was that surely it was against regulations. He was about to speak when he noticed her looking at him.

"Spartan, you okay there?" she said with a smirk.

He stood for a moment, a little surprised before regaining his composure.

"Of course, what are you doing here? You're not in this platoon, are you?"

"Haven't you noticed you're down a man? Apparently, somebody has been getting a bit physical in the close quarter combat classes and they needed somebody new, I'm a replacement for your platoon. I volunteered." She smiled at him as he laughed.

"Ah, I see. Am I supposed to be flattered?"

Teresa turned back to the shower, letting the water run over her face for a little longer before turning back to him.

"Maybe."

"Anyway, how is the training going? We have Harris,

he's got a major hard on for bayonets," she asked as she brought the subject back to their training.

"Yeah, same for us, these guys do like their little knives! We've done some marksmanship with the training rifles and loads of physical training."

Teresa came out from under the shower, moving a little closer to Spartan. "Physical training, huh?"

The buzzer on the wall indicated the end of their shower. The water cut abruptly with just warm steam spreading through the room.

"L48 Rifle training to start in eight minutes," came the voice before the system went silent.

The recruits left the shower area, drying themselves and getting dressed. Teresa and Spartan stood at the end of the block. Teresa noticed some of the scarring running down Spartan's back.

"God, what caused that?"

Spartan stopped and tried to work out where she was looking. "Which one?" he asked, finding it difficult to identify the exact injury.

Teresa reached out and ran her hand along a scar from his shoulder to his ribs. Her unexpected contact made him jump a little.

"Ah, yeah, that one. It was from one of my last fights before I volunteered." He put extra special emphasis on the last word.

"What kind of weapon could have done it?" she asked,

genuinely interested.

"You'd be surprised, it was a blunt mace fitted with dull studs. It wasn't supposed to cut the flesh, that was supposed to be part of the deal but somebody, I don't know who rigged the fight and replaced the stubs with small spikes."

"Christ! How did you get out of that one?" she asked as she pulled on her top.

"Well, at first I didn't. The wound was massive but the guy was cocky. He made the mistake of getting too close to check on his handiwork."

"I take it you explained this to him?" She stood there grinning at him.

Spartan looked away and at the recruits leaving the room, he took in a deep breath, remembering the bloody fight and the injuries involved. It was strange, at the time he had hated every single minute of it, but now that he looked back to the events just months ago he almost missed the action.

"Something like that."

* * *

It had taken over a month for the CCS Santa Maria to make her way around the storms that surrounded the planet Prometheus. Spartan had heard the Marine Corps actively recruited from the gangs and captured criminals.

In fact it was the only reason the ship made the dangerous journey, to collect the toughest and most violent men in the Proxima System. Apparently now they were in open space the vessel spent most of its time coasting so that training could begin. They could fire up the engines and be anywhere in the sector in no more than a few weeks but they had another dozen stops and new recruits arrived with each new planet or station they passed by. Spartan barely noticed any of this though, he was determined to make amends and if this meant being a Marine then he was damned sure he was going to be the best!

Training had now progressed to the firearms stage and Spartan was starting to feel the competition. Unlike most of the recruits, he had little experience with shooting and actually found the action of waiting and taking careful aim to be less than exciting. All of his combat experience had been in the brutal close quarter brawling of the illegal pit fights. In those fights it was all about individual combat, fighting skill and attitude. There were few that could face him in a fight and expect to win, but that didn't involve the use of firearms. This was a total change for him and he was having a problem getting around to the idea that even the weakest, most inexperienced recruit could bring him down with a standard issue firearm.

The Drill Sergeant was certainly not going any easier on them. But at least he seemed to have a minor measure of respect for the improvements in discipline and close quarter combat they had worked on. They had already been issued with their weapons, though it had been made clear from the start that they were being loaded with safe ammunition that would cause no more than bruises.

This was the largest training hall on the ship and reinforced with three layers on the outer hull proofed against all the weapons they used. Even if anything did go wrong there was an additional section fitted outside, but that had apparently never happened. They had already trained in this section and the space was big enough to conduct anything up to platoon-sized actions, with or without weapons. Now, the one end was equipped as a firing range although Spartan had seen it previously equipped as a mock village and tunnel sequence for use by the recruits.

The Sergeant stepped forward and held a weapon up in front of him.

"This here is the L48 rifle. It is the standard ranged weapon of every marine and you will carry it wherever you go. It is available in both rifle and carbine versions. The default round is 12.7mm, this makes it a large calibre weapon but with improvements in recoil reduction, you will notice almost no different to the 10mm training round. The selector will choose proximity modes on the bullets giving you flexibility in combat. As with every marine rifle the M11 bayonet will easily fit without affecting the balance of the weapon." He walked down the line.

"Each magazine carries twenty rounds of variable operation ammunition. You will not waste these. In combat, you must make every round count. If you need greater firepower, we still have the modular 6mm module that will allow you to fit the smaller calibre box magazine to both the rifle and carbine variants. These are recommended for close quarter assault roles only or for use in sealed environments where armour penetration could be a problem. For most occasions, you will want the flexibility of the new 12.7mm VO rounds. These will give you the most tactical advantages." He held up one of the rounds.

"Now, watch carefully whilst I demonstrate the use of this damned fine piece of equipment!"

He lifted the rifle to his shoulder and aimed down the range. At the far end was a line of cardboard shapes that looked very roughly man sized. He squeezed the trigger and fired a single round. There was a muffled report as the round blasted from the weapon and smashed straight through the target's head leaving a milk bottle-sized hole.

"Now, that was the standard mode and uses none of the advantages of the new VO rounds. The next mode is what we call armour-penetrating mode. It will trigger a small explosive blast at a distance of one metre behind the first object it strikes. This means you can put a round through a wall or lightly armoured vehicle and still take out the man inside," he said with a wry grin.

The Sergeant flicked the selector on the side and fired again at the next target. This time there was a sheet with a gap behind and then another target set up. The round ripped through the first as before and then a short distance behind spread a cloud of silver dust on the target.

"Obviously we do not use live weapons, unless we want to get blasted into space. Now don't worry too much. From what I have been following you will get plenty of opportunity to put these weapons to the test against our Zealot friends."

Turning back to the range, he flicked the switch to the last mode.

"Now, this is the pièce de résistance for the L48. For those of you with the IQ of a drainpipe that means this is the single best feature of this great weapon."

A dull grumble spread through the group though it was a fair split down the middle, half unimpressed with the criticism, the rest not quite sure what had just been said.

"What do you do when Z-Man is hiding in a bunker or building of some kind? Sure, you could pop a round through the wall but that assumes you can penetrate it. The L48 is good but it isn't magic. Reinforced concrete and heavy armour can stop a weapon but this guy can hit round a corner."

A murmur of surprise continued through the group.

"Just watch!" The Sergeant swung the weapon around. At the far end of the hall was a mock wall with a small window beyond which was another target. The Sergeant waved his hand and one of his assistants pushed the man-shaped target down into a crouching position so that it couldn't be seen through the window.

"Note how our cowardly foe keeps his head down so we can't hit him. Well, tough shit pal!" He pulled the trigger. The gun fired and from their perspective the students could see a cloud of silver dust behind the wall. The Sergeant signalled to his assistant who then lowered the wall so the recruits could see the target covered in powder.

"What you see here is the laser rangefinder capability being integrated with the advanced projectile. The way this works is simple. Aim for the outer wall that your guy is hiding behind. Hit the range button, this will set the sight for your weapon. Then hit the armour penetration mode, the same mode you used at the start. The shell will explode one metre behind the range you selected. Recruits, to your places!"

They spread out into the twelve places designated for the marksmen. Spartan lay down in the third and checked his weapon as he had been taught. The gun was certainly far from new but it appeared intact and nothing was broken or missing, as far as he could tell. He checked the chamber was clear and the magazine was out of the weapon. One final check ensured the gun was on safety before he put up his hand to signal he was ready.

"This will be a precision round. Each of you has a twelve-round training magazine. You will be presented with a random selection of targets and will have to choose the correct weapon mode to claim the kill. Once you take out the target the next will load in automatically. There are ten targets, that gives you two spare. I want to see spare rounds by the end of the shooting. Understood?"

"Yes, Sergeant!" came the chorus in response.

"Make ready!"

The targets loaded into position, the first being a simple man-sized target, nothing fancy. The recruits readied their guns, aiming carefully but waiting for the signal.

"Fire!"

A volley of fire like that of a Napoleonic battle erupted down the line as the guns fired in unison. Every single target was knocked down and the second targets moved in to replace them. This time they faced the man behind a wall. The change in target resulted in a few of them pausing whilst they considered what to do, followed by a ragged volley of gunshots. Only half of the targets changed and it became instantly clear that it was a trick round. The figures behind the walls were positioned off to one side. Only those that selected the armour-penetrating mode, or the laser rangefinder with the extra metre selected, hit the man first time. It was all a bit confusing.

Spartan was having fun and so far he'd hit two out of two, he seemed to be in the top few of the group. The third target popped up, it was two men, one next to the other. Without thinking he fired one round then another. As the target dropped a bunker appeared. It seemed to only take about thirty seconds and the shooting was over.

"Clear your weapons and show me what you have left!" The Sergeant shouted.

Each of the recruits made their weapons safe and then ejected the spare training rounds from the chamber and magazine. Of the twelve recruits only one had two spare rounds, the rest were a mixture.

The Sergeant walked along the line, stopping at each recruit, berating them for their shooting. When he reached Spartan he looked less than impressed.

"What is this?" he asked sarcastically.

Spartan had the weapon laid out before him but with no spare rounds.

"I hit them all, Sergeant," answered Spartan, though he was starting to realise he had done something wrong.

The Sergeant moved to the next shooter, it was the ginger-haired man from the incident when he first arrived. The man held up two rounds.

"I'd be so impressed if you'd actually hit the ten targets, look again."

The recruits all looked down the range to find one of the targets still standing. As they watched, the Sergeant whipped out his pistol and fired a single shot down the line, striking the head of the target. It fell back and the course was finally complete. The Sergeant moved back to Spartan.

"You wasted rounds on targets that one round could easily have done. Remember number three? The one with two guys stood close together?"

Spartan nodded, realising what was coming.

"You fired at each. Why not used the timed-mode with range finder? One shot, two kills. The round can easily take out three or four targets in one go. That means a shot like Ginger here can still get kills even if he misses. You understand?"

"Yes, Sergeant!" answered Spartan.

The Drill Sergeant turned to the ginger man and raised his eyebrow.

"Uh, yes, Sergeant!" he added, looking a little sheepish.

"Back in line, next group front and centre, let's see if you can do any better!"

As Spartan moved back in line, he walked past Teresa who moved to take his position. As they passed she gave him a single raised eyebrow. He turned his head and watched her as she moved into place and lifted the rifle to her shoulder.

SIEGE OF TITAN

CHAPTER FIVE

The Centauri Confederacy at its height consisted of three star systems, scores of colonised planets and hundreds of moons. The first to be colonised was Alpha Centauri, two stars, and after decades of exploitation, it had become the industrial and commercial heart of the confederation. The Proxima Centauri was the next major system to be colonised by humanity following the great expansion but also the greatest in terms of population and development.

The jewel of the system was the planet named Prime, the largest planet in the Confederation. Colonised in the image of old Earth it was the most populous planet and boasted a lifestyle that centuries before would have been idealised as the utopian dream of plenty.

Proxima Prime

The rec room was packed as the recruits spent their limited free time relaxing and chatting before moving on to yet another drill or exercise. The room was about twenty metres long and contained chairs, a few tables on one side and a set of computer displays. A steady batch of recruits took turns to make use of the time to contact loved ones or simply chat to anybody other than the same faces they saw every day.

Spartan, Jesus, Marcus and Teresa were sitting around one of the tables. Marcus and Jesus were arguing whilst the others looked on in amusement.

"Bullshit, little man." Marcus laughed as he spun his computer tablet in front of him. "No way can a man in this old metal armour be able to move and fight like that, no dammed way!"

Jesus waved his hand and brought up a video sequence showing a man in a substantial metal suit of armour. He was covered from head to toe and wielded a huge sword that was almost as tall as the man himself.

"Look, it says here the armoured knight could fight on foot or horseback and that the sword was well balanced, agile and could even be held in the middle when fighting armour," said Jesus.

"Look, you put that much metal on a man and all you can do is just stand there and not get hurt. I'd bet good money that most of that gear is ceremonial shit, nothing to do with combat."

Teresa frowned at them both before turning to Spartan.

"You've used more armour than anybody else, what do you think?"

Jesus spun the tablet around so Spartan could get a good look at the armour. He examined it in detail, moving the image around so he could see it from all sides and even zooming in to look at the thickness.

"Yeah, it could be done," he said dismissively.

"Ok, genius, would you like to expand on that?" asked a dubious Marcus.

"Not really," said a grinning Spartan.

"So we should just take your word for it then?"

"You should, Jesus, but something tells me you're not going to."

"Come on, man, tell us why you think this huge lump of metal is anything more than some fancy outfit for a rich dude." Jesus said as he settled back into his chair.

"Don't make the assumption that just because this gear is old it wasn't designed for a purpose. Some armour is ceremonial, other is for combat and some armour fits somewhere in the middle. Armour has been used since biblical times and we're still using it today."

"Nice speech, granddad. Is that it?"

"Alright, Marcus, if you insist." He took in a lung full of air.

"Look at the armour first of all. Yes, it has embellishments but not overly so. The joints are in the same places we have for our personal armour. The thickness of the metal is much less than you would expect for something designed to protect your body. Look at the fluting, the angles and the extra plating to protect the joints. See the vulnerable gaps, like the armpit, there's extra flexible chainmail. This is the work of a man, maybe many men that are expert craftsmen and experts in their trade." He moved away from the image and then displayed another similar suit of armour.

"Look at this one. It is a little later and much less ornate. The description here says it's munitions grade armour. That is basically the equivalent of the kind of stuff we have. Note all the joints and plates are in the same place. Yes, the metal isn't as pretty and it doesn't have the fancy fittings, but to all intents and purposes it does exactly the same job."

"Yeah, so you say. But what about in practice? Can you move, duck and cut with a weapon wearing that."

"Why not, Marcus? When I was fighting we used all kinds of armour. Back then it was just as important to put on a good display as it was to protect parts of the body. When you are fighting for your life you will push yourself further than at any other time. Yes, armour and padding will slow you down and wear you out, but you practice as much as possible to reduce the problem. I've worn body armour that probably weighed a lot more than anything you've shown me there. As for that weapon, look at the blade and at the craftsmanship. Don't assume for a moment that it wasn't a deadly weapon."

He leaned back with a look of self-satisfaction. Teresa smiled but added nothing as she watched Marcus and Jesus for their reactions.

"Yeah, if you say so. The weapon, come on, no fucking way!" Marcus said.

"In my experience weapons are very much designed around the kind of enemy you expect to face. If you're fighting unarmoured people then something that can cut will work fine. If they are wearing thicker clothing or armour you'll need something that is better for penetration. A spear point will pierce armour more easily than the edge of a sword, also don't forget," he added before being interrupted.

A loud sound came from the end of the room followed by a commotion as though somebody had just dropped something valuable. Spartan instantly stopped talking and turned to the direction of the noise.

"Hey, have you seen this?" came a cry from the end of the rec room.

A number of the recruits started to move to the end with just a few of them staying where they were. One woman waved her hands as she accessed visual feeds and then moved a selection to the entire section of the shorter wall. The video feeds split up into one large view plus a dozen smaller ones, all showing the latest news feeds.

Spartan and Teresa joined them, Jesus stood up on his chair to look over the crowd. With the amount of noise from the recruits Spartan couldn't make out the voice on the report. He moved closer, brushing aside the few people not listening.

"The fuckers have captured Titan Naval Station! They are saying it is another Pearl Harbor!" shouted one of the men excitedly.

"No way, man, that's bullshit!" replied another.

"Who?" Yet another shouted.

"The Zealots, they've done it this time, they've hit the biggest naval station in the sector! How the fuck can we get to the planet if they've taken control of Titan?" cried a tall man in the middle of the crowd.

Spartan was now close enough and could see the story for himself. The video showed the massive base, along the top and bottom the scrolling ticker detailed facts and figures. The first to catch his attention was that it confirmed terrorists had captured the loading station and dock. Even more worrying was the section that explained how three transports, one of them a massive cargo vessel, had been crashed in a massive suicide attack on the naval facilities there crippling several vessels, as well as destroying much of the marine barracks.

"That's our biggest station in the system. Last I heard there were about two million people there," Spartan said.

"Not just the people, that's the home of the local fleet,

it's our drop-off point in less than a month for fuck's sake. They're saying the terrorists have crippled the Resolution and taken control of Victorious, that's a fucking battleship, man!" Someone called out.

"That isn't possible," said Teresa, "no way could a ship that big be taken over by half-trained terrorists."

She turned her tablet around and brought up a rotating image of the warship. Along the one side were columns of data. "Come on, it says there are always at least three hundred marines on board the Victorious as well as her crew."

"Maybe they had help from the inside?" suggested Jesus.

"There must be other ships in the area!" Marcus suggested.

Spartan moved nearer to one of the secondary displays and scrolled though more stories. His heart was pounding because one thing experience had taught him was that when things went wrong, they usually ended up on his lap. On the second screen, he had the official information from Naval Intelligence that confirmed much of what was in the news. It was incredible. He took a few breaths before turning back to Marcus and Teresa. As he started to speak a number of the other recruits crowded in to listen.

"The latest Intel confirms that the fighting on Proxima Prime has expanded to the eleven transit stations and that a full scale rebellion at the Titan Naval Station is underway. One Admiral has either been assassinated or may be involved. The shipyard was hit first, then the garrison. A dozen ships escaped but several warships are unaccounted for and they are holding over one thousand military personnel hostage on the Station.

"What about the civilians?" asked one of the recruits.

"Some managed to escape on freighters and ferry vessels but most are still trapped there."

"No way, man, no fucking way!" Jesus was watching the burning buildings on the main screen. The volume was turned up so they could hear the story from the reporters at the scene.

"Three hours ago over a dozen co-ordinated attacks in the capital destroyed the parliament building and the central stock exchange. Fires are still burning at the headquarters of the Council Chambers," said the voice.

"Fuck me, did you see the residential zone?" asked Teresa.

Jesus stepped to one of the small feeds and moved back to the cameras pointing into the residential area. On this part of the city were scores of tower blocks, some reaching nearly two hundred metres tall and featuring beautiful spires pointing up in the sky. One of the buildings was ablaze and the top third of another had collapsed. The ticker along the bottom said over eight hundred people were trapped in the burning building.

As the recruits watched a series of additional explosions ripped across the city as more buildings were hit until columns of smoke and bright flashes could be seen in all directions. Overhead a multitude of rescue craft rushed around, landing on buildings to evacuate people while others were trying to fight the fires.

The door to the room opened and in walked the Drill Sergeant. The recruits all stood to attention though nobody remembered to switch off the displays. He marched in, flanked by two of his men. As he moved along the room he stopped and stared at the displays, the glow of the fires reflecting on his face before he gave a hand gesture to his two marines. They moved forward and deactivated them, throwing the area into silence.

"You have all seen we are in a real situation here. As of one hour ago the insurgents on Proxima Prime announced their intentions to spread a holy war through every moon and colony in the Confederation. So far it has spread to most of the cities on the planet and three Titan Stations, including Titan Naval Station. This is serious shit, if Confed doesn't respond fast we could be cut off from Proxima Prime and that leaves the civilians completely exposed."

One of the marines at his side passed him a tablet that was glowing with scrolling data and images. He looked at it and then at the recruits.

"As of fifteen minutes ago Confed military forces

have been put on full alert. This policing action has been officially designated a warzone and we are in the damned middle. The Zealots have been declared enemy combatants and we are authorised to use all weapons and forces at our disposal to end this emergency, once and for all! Today is the first day of the Proxima Emergency and we will see it through to the end!"

Several of the recruits cheered but most were silent, waiting for the rest of his news, each convinced that there was something much bigger and much worse waiting for them.

"When you joined most of you were going to end up on the front lines fighting on the northern continent of Prime. It was supposed to be the last stronghold of this bastardised radicalised movement. We've been treating this as a glorified policing action to keep the civilians calm and the politicians happy. Bullshit! It hasn't worked and now it is spreading fast. We were wrong, seriously wrong," he said ominously.

He started to pace in front of the assembled Marines.

"We should have learnt our lesson from the last war, religion and politics breeds problems. You all know what happened with Carthago and Terra Nova don't you?"

The recruits fidgeted, uncomfortable at the question and not one lifted their hands. The Drill Instructor looked as though he was about to blow a fuse when Teresa spoke.

"My family are from Carthago, Sir."

He marched up and stopped directly in front of her, examining her carefully from head to toe.

"Name?"

"Recruit Teresa Morato, Sir!"

"Tell me, what do you know about the last war? Who started it?"

"I, uh, I don't know, Sir. It was something to do with colonisation of Proxima I think."

The Drill Instructor appeared to relax slightly in front of the marines.

"Exactly. The problems started when the two largest colonies, the conservative farming planet Carthago and the industrious Terra Nova, disagreed on colonising Proxima. The arguments were long and complicated but it ended with their friends and allies fighting though the System. This has happened many times in the past. The main factions sit back and let their allies do the work until one day, when the tide starts to turn, the two big players have to wade in."

"Tell me, Recruit Morato. How would you describe Carthago today, after all the years of war and strife?"

"It is a poor planet. Most of the cities were levelled in the Great War and many are still in a bad way. There are frequent terrorist actions and it is the most violent colony outside of the stations around Prometheus."

"What about religion?"

"Most are underground and meet in secret. The major

sects were banned or abandoned the colony during the exodus after the war."

The Drill Instructor stood upright and looked around the group for anyone else.

"Who has been to Terra Nova?"

Several hands went up and like a lurcher he moved in to one of the nervous looking men at the back.

"Name?"

"Recruit John Jenkins, Sir."

"You look pretty, you a Doctor or something?" he asked sarcastically.

"My family run a factory on Terra. I studied there before enlisting, Sir."

The Drill Instructor shook his head in despair.

"Look what my beloved Corps has been forced to turn to. Tell me, Recruit Jenkins, what is Terra Nova like?"

"It is the richest and most cosmopolitan colony in the Confederacy. There are people and money and all kinds of opportunities."

"Religion?"

"It is practiced but not the same as on Carthago. It is more of a meditation circle or social club on Terra. The old religions of Carthago are thought to be barbaric and ancient, religions for the common, bestial man."

The Drill Instructor nodded in agreement.

"There you have it. Even today we have different people, different values and religion is at the core. The biggest mistake we made was driving the old religions underground. Now we can see they are stronger, more numerous and violent than before. Look at Terra Nova. Peaceful, soft and rich while the angry and backward world of Carthago continues to rot. This is the world you are about to face. It is cruel and full of intolerance. You will be Marines and you will uphold the traditions and values of the Corps and the Confederacy that thousands died to create. Do you get me?"

"We get you Sir!" came the chorus back to him.

He walked along the recruits, looking at each of them in turn with a look of satisfaction on his face.

"Every one of you has passed basic training and you are already three-quarters though the commando course. You have done well, damned well and I would be proud to take any of you into action with me."

The group were obviously surprised, this being the first praise they'd ever heard from him.

"We have changed course and will be meeting with the Fleet assembling on the Rim. We will arrive in less than a week. After that we head for the Titan stations and the war. I can't tell you how long this fight will go on for or how difficult it will be. What I can tell you is that in one week, whether you like it or not, you will be marines and you will be baptised in fire and finally earn your title of marines!"

A cheer rang out through the room as the Sergeant

paced back and forth. It went on for almost a minute before he ordered them to stop.

"I don't know the exact details yet but I do know that Confed will aim to stop this revolt and fast. The Titan stations control all access to Prime and if we lose Prime we lose the most important planet in the entire System. I need you to work hard and get yourselves ready. Whatever you've been doing, do more. Only some of you will have completed the full commando training but that isn't going to keep you from combat. I will be assigning those of you that pass the course specific duties when the time comes but for now remember, every marine is a rifleman and you will perform your duty the same as every other marine.

"You will all assemble in the aft training hall in thirty minutes, it is time for your zero-g squad exercise and based on the news you have all just heard you are going to want to get lots of zero-g time in. This will be the up-scaled version of last week's exercise. There is already a full company of recruits from Bravo Company getting dug in. It will be your job to clear the training course of all hostiles with minimal casualties. Full briefing in thirty minutes."

He walked to the door and turned back.

"Hoorah!" he shouted, instantly followed by an enthusiastic response from the recruits.

* * *

Lieutenant Erdeniz sat in his quarters reading the reports that were still coming in about the attacks on Proxima. He had family in the capital but after four hours of nearly continuous effort, he couldn't make contact through any of the regular channels. Less news was getting out from the main communication satellites, whether that was due to weather, technical or hostile actions he couldn't tell. The last message from the centre of the capital said the city was under martial law and the Army were clearing the streets. The briefing with the command staff had confirmed that the CCS Crusader was heading to the Rim to meet with as many ships as could be mobilised.

Reports indicated that the Titan Naval Station was now under insurgent control and protected by over twenty vessels, though this was not confirmed. It also said that the smaller orbiting transit stations had been attacked but it wasn't clear if all or some were now under insurgent control. Either way Prime was being blockaded and it would be hard, if not impossible, to get to the planet's surface or to escape without facing attack by vessels waiting at the stations. Confed had been seriously caught with their pants down this time, and as usual, it would fall to people like him to pick up the pieces.

The rumble of the engines was much more prominent than normal and he could feel it through the deck. He had only thirty minutes break before he was to return to the gun decks for additional testing and practice. The Captain had already informed them that action was imminent and that this would be the first time the Fleet had been used in anger in over thirty years. Although his room was deep inside the vessel, he did have a virtual window that gave the illusion of facing the hull of the ship. He could make out the infinite number of stars and he thought to himself how wondrous it would be to be able to travel fast enough to visit them. So far, no vessels had been able to travel faster than light. There were still plenty of books and movies being made based upon the assumption it would happen but after many generations nothing had changed. The journey from Earth to Alpha Centauri still took just under ten years and though the transports still plied their way between the old and the new world, it wasn't fast enough for them to expand into the real recesses of deep space.

The sound of his door alarm buzzed and he pressed the intercom button without even taking his eyes off the screen.

"Ensign Harris here, Sir, I have the firing results for you."

Erdeniz hit the button and the door slid open neatly. In walked the Ensign with his computer tablet in his hands. His uniform was a little scruffy and Erdeniz was already feeling irritable when he saw the man enter.

"You could have sent it to my account you know!"

"Yes, Sir, I needed to bring you something else though."

"Really?" he replied sarcastically.

There was something strange about Harris he thought, his face looked clammy and there was something else, yes, the real difference was in his demeanour. He always appeared subservient to authority but for some reason he looked as if he hadn't a care in the world. Erdeniz put it down to the stress or concern of the upcoming action with the insurgents. He made to reach forward to take the tablet when he noticed something on the Ensign's foot. He looked closer, noticing the dark red stain. It looked like fortified wine or maybe blood. He smiled to himself as he though of claret and its double meaning before it dawned on him.

"What happened to your foot?" he asked though his pulse was already telling him something very bad was about to happen.

The Ensign looked directly at Erdeniz, his expression changing to anger or more likely contempt. He remembered the look from his micro expression classes during his psychology modules. It was the look of a man who was suddenly showing his true feelings and they were like nothing he had ever experienced face to face before. He recoiled slightly at the man's expression.

"Shit!" he muttered as he reached for the alarm on the wall.

The Ensign rushed forward, drawing a roughly made blade from inside his tunic. The blade was narrow, almost like a stiletto. It had the look of a weapon that had been fabricated from something on the ship. It certainly wasn't military issue. It had no discernable edges but did have a vicious point that could probably penetrate even the thickest clothing. It was like a cross between a stiletto and a prison made shiv.

With the weapon held high he jumped forward, covering the distance in no time at all and stabbed hard. As he moved he cried out, shrieking in some unintelligible language. Erdeniz reacted quickly but it wasn't quick enough and as he turned the blade struck him in the shoulder. The pain was excruciating and he screamed out at the same time as hitting the button. The alarm triggered immediately as he slumped to the floor. The blade had penetrated its entire length and blood was already pouring profusely from the wound. He tried to move but something heavy smashed into the side of his head and he found himself lying on the floor. The room started to blur and he was convinced he was dying.

"Get up you idiot!" he shouted in his mind, desperately trying to keep his eyes open, not wanting to give the man the opportunity to finish him off.

The pain was agonising but he kept at it, finally able to roll onto his front and reached around to the blade. As he turned, he half expected the next final blow but the Ensign was busy rummaging through his personal terminal, scrolling through his classified data. Erdeniz reached to his thigh and clicked open the holster, withdrew his sidearm and pointed it at the Ensign.

"Get back from the terminal, Ensign!"

He tried to stand but the pain ripped though his body, the knife still jammed into his body. The Ensign ignored him and continued to work on the computer. Erdeniz flipped the button on his pistol that automatically loaded in a ship safe round. The rubber tipped round could easily kill an unarmoured man at this range and there was no possibility it could penetrate the skin of any part of the ship or damage the major circuits or equipment inside. Hearing the noise from the gun Harris turned and looked directly at him. He snarled and then ran at Erdeniz, taking him by surprise.

"Fuck me!" he cried as he fumbled with the pistol. The man was on him by the time he'd collected his senses and as the two fell backwards he emptied every round from the pistol into the charging man. As they crashed into his desk items flew everywhere and his head smacked hard on the metal frame. This time he didn't get back up as the blackness closed in on him.

* * *

Spartan and Marcus used their thrusters to move towards the access hatch. As they hit the button on their suits, small puffs of gases ejected from the suits' miniscule exhausts and helped them manoeuvre in precise detail. These were generally used by engineering crews working on the outside of ships but sometimes also by marines when conducting boarding operations or working on the outside of stations in zero-g gravity situations.

The training area was a massive purpose built environment that used to be a storage compartment for materials and supplies. The total size was similar to a football ground and big enough to conduct detailed combat scenarios in a gravity free situation. The current layout matched the access sections of the Titan Naval Station and contained mock airlocks, shafts and rooms. Their platoon had split into three squads, each of twelve men. They had already taken a number of casualties trying to reach the cover of the structure. The defenders had set up secure firing positions so they could cover access points to the base.

Marcus reached out, holding onto the metal railings near the airlock hatch and attached the override mechanism. All the recruits in the other two squads were wearing their standard Personal Defence Suits along with their manoeuvring modules. Spartan and his squad had swapped their gear for the combat engineer rig. These suits were much thicker and bulkier than the usual armour but they were also equipped with heavy-duty hydraulic gear and close range weapons. Spartan moved to the side of the door and slammed the armoured fist like a battering ram into the metal.

"What are you doing, man, I'm nearly done!" Marcus shouted through the intercom.

He struck the metal three more times before he had ripped open a hole big enough to use his other fist on. Just a few more pulls and he had torn open a hole that was wide enough to go through.

"Keep on the door, old man, I wouldn't be surprised if they've mined it," he said with a grin.

Teresa and Marcus followed him inside the shaft and lowered themselves to the side so they could activate their grav boots. These gave them grip on the metal surface but they had to be careful, there were plenty of items they wouldn't stick to and there was still the lack of gravity to contend with.

A volley of rubber tipped bullets rushed down the corridor, silent in the vacuum of space. Several of them struck Marcus but the impact failed to register. His heavy cutting tools absorbed the impact.

"You see what I meant earlier? This suit has three times the protection on the front. Perfect for boarding actions."

"Yes, nice, I can see that, Spartan!" Marcus said, he couldn't stop a little smile escaping.

The shaft shook and Spartan could see three recruits drifting from one of the other access hatches, a series of sparks and smoke indicating the door had blown out with an improvised charge.

Teresa banged her armoured hand against the side of the shaft as he shouted. "Nice work! Looks like it's just us left then."

Jesus entered the shaft and activated his boots, following him were four more recruits, the rest had been picked off on the way in.

"Damn, we lost four then, trying to get here," said Spartan to himself. "This is Charlie Squad, anybody from Alpha or Bravo still in action?" he asked over the secure communications channel.

"Two of us are pinned down near the medical station, rest of my squad is wasted!" came a familiar voice, he was sure it was Burnett.

"That you, Burnett, who else is with you?"

There was a pause for a few seconds, "Just me and Matt."

Spartan looked at Teresa and Marcus who grinned back at him.

"Hang in there, stay in cover, we're coming from the loading airlock."

The heavy suits were slow, much slower than the normal suits, but there was nothing they could do to speed things up. As they reached a few metres from the half-open door ahead two recruits popped their head outs and opened fire. Marcus leaned to the side lowering his left arm to reveal a very quick modification he had done. He'd strapped the three L48 rifles that he, Spartan and Teresa had been issued with to the metal mountings and run a cable inside his suit. He had also fitted the optional small calibre, close assault module and ammunition boxes. It was ridiculous overkill but the result was mightily impressive. He pulled the trigger and the three weapons opened fire with their small calibre rounds.

It was a surreal sight as the rapid flashes signalled the discharge of the silent weapons. Hundreds of rubber tipped rounds blasted through the shaft and easily hit the recruits as well as another two that were moving in to reinforce them. Even funnier was that the bullets forced the recruits backwards and along the shaft as they lost their grip.

"Yeah!" Spartan shouted, as he pushed ahead and into the junction room that led to different parts of the station.

He stomped ahead to the shaft directly ahead. With this route now secure, the four new arrivals each in their normal armour made quick progress into the shafts and proceeded to move in on the enemy command room. By splitting apart the four recruits would be able to strike the target area from four directions. Marcus and Teresa moved up to the flanks of Spartan.

"I'm receiving complaints from the defenders that some of you are ignoring your hits," came a voice over the intercom, it was the Drill Sergeant.

"Bullshit, the front armour on these suits is proof for twenty millimetre anti-tank rounds," said Spartan abruptly.

"Indeed, somebody has done their homework, continue," came the reply.

"Spartan Unit in position," Marcus said with a sly smile.

"Spartan Unit? You kidding?" Teresa laughed.

Spartan looked at them both, turning his head before looking back at the last door. He spoke quietly. "On the other side of this door is a ten metre shaft that leads directly into the Command Centre. Jesus, give us the word when your team is in position."

Jesus was positioned a short distance away and moving to follow the four other recruits. He turned giving a hand signal as he disappeared into one of the small shafts.

Spartan lifted his armoured arms in front of the suit. Because of the tools and hydraulics, as well as the added armour, it was like a complicated heavy metal shield that could easily protect the wearer from most of the incoming fire. Teresa did the same, pushing the metal in front of them for protection.

"We're in position," came the message from Jesus.

Spartan nodded, looking at the two standing next to him.

"Okay, I rip open the door then we push the armour forward. As we distract them, you drop in on the flanks and take them out one at a time. Remember, single shots, keep in cover and take them out. Understood?"

A chorus of affirmative gave him his answer. Spartan slowly pushed the hatch forward with his hands, knowing the door may be rigged with a charge. He pushed the blades from his hand into the metal wrenching the side of the hatch away. As the door drifted off he was surprised to find no charges set.

"Bet they left it open for us to walk into," said Teresa as she looked about for the enemy.

"Follow me!" Spartan pushed ahead and into the shaft.

They followed Spartan closely, both looking for signs of trouble. Marcus brought up the rear and ensured they weren't attacked from behind.

As soon as they reached the end of the shaft they were in the Command Centre. Literally as soon as Spartan's foot clunked into place, the room lit up with the muzzle flashes of the dozen surviving recruits. Round after ineffectual round clattered off their armour. Teresa moved up to Spartan's left and raised her arms, deflecting most of the rounds from her thickly armoured suit.

"Now!" Spartan shouted.

It was over almost as soon as it had begun. The hatches in four different places popped open and flashes of movement indicated the rounds blasting the survivors. In just five seconds, the defenders were out of the fight. The avalanche of fire stopped and everything seemed to stop moving.

"Jesus, take your unit and get Burnett and Matt secured." Spartan ordered.

"Affirmative."

Back in the Command Centre, the three recruits moved inside, checking for survivors. The so-called killed defenders kept to the sides and out of the way of the exercise. Spartan saw a reflection and made to move his hand when Teresa spotted movement behind them. She moved quickly, looking to place her heavy frontal armour between Spartan and the enemy but she wasn't fast enough. As the men opened fire though Marcus intercepted them. He was slightly to the side and had been checking one of the hatches. He opened fire with his improvised assault arm that was still fitted with the modified weapons and hit the two attackers with over a hundred rounds.

A light flashed inside Spartan's suit, indicating a hit to a valve. A computerised voice spoke, indicating he had suffered a critical hit.

"Cease fire. End of exercise!" came the order over the intercom. "All recruits report to the briefing room in thirty minutes for debrief, out!"

"Man, that guy needs to learn to lower his blood pressure!" said Marcus.

The three looked at each other, only Spartan's suit failure light flashed.

"Well, two out of three isn't bad," Teresa said.

The briefing room was packed with the exhausted recruits. The competitors sat together, but apart. It was incredible how one group of people could feel as much friends as they were enemies. That was the price of competition Spartan thought to himself.

The Drill Sergeant entered the room and marched up in front of them.

"That was an interesting exercise and I'm pleased to say some of you survived to tell the tale. The defender team suffered one hundred percent casualties. That is thirty-two out of thirty-two killed in action. Before you get excited, only nine survived from the attackers but that is still damned fine odds for this mission."

He walked along the line, looking at each of them in turn before stopping.

"Will the survivors please stand up."

Two groups of people stood up, Burnett and Matt at one end and Spartan's group at the other.

"Now look here, nine recruits, nine fighters, some of whom probably wanted to slam the others' heads against the bulkhead managed to achieve a total victory against an enemy that was dug into a superior position. Outstanding!"

He continued walking along the front of the group, this time paying attention to those standing.

"What's your name, marine?" he asked.

Some of the recruits looked at each other in surprise, it was the first time they had heard him use that word.

"Teresa Martinez, Sergeant!" The Drill Sergeant extended his hand and shook hers before turning to the rest of the group.

"This marine performed above and beyond the call. She

used initiative, overcame difficulties and even put herself in the line of fire for another marine. I could ask no more of any one of you. Hoorah!" he shouted with a smile.

The rest of the recruits stood, shouting in congratulation to the survivors and the sense that on that day they had in part, achieved some measure of respect from their Sergeant.

"You earned yourselves a day's leave. In twenty-four hours you undergo your final test. Those of you who pass will become a marine. Some of you, if you score highly enough, will even join the commandos. Dismissed!"

The recruits filed out of the hall and headed in different directions, some to their quarters and others to the two recreation rooms. Unlike previous training activities, this one seemed to have encouraged them to intermingle as the recruits swapped stories on the complex operation they'd just worked through.

Spartan, Jesus, and Marcus walked down the main corridor towards their usual rec room. As they passed the first set of berths, Teresa appeared at the doorway.

"Hey, Spartan!"

He walked up to the door, placing one hand on the bulkhead.

"Inside!" she shouted with a grin.

Reaching out she grabbed Spartan and yanked him so he fell through the open door. As he stumbled to the floor she slammed the door shut.

Marcus looked at Jesus with a look of surprise on his face.

"Bastard!" laughed Jesus.

CHAPTER SIX

When the first colonists arrived on Prime they built several small outposts on the more habitable moons. The greatest of all was built on the moon Kronus, named after mighty Greek Titan. As the planet below was colonised a number of further manmade transit stations were built so that ships, people and materials could be moved freely to and from the planet.

Following their role in the Great War, each of the twelve stations was improved with extra ports, habitation sections, defences and garrisons. The moon of Kronus with its low gravity, thick atmosphere and abundance of raw materials became the Titan Naval Station. This was the largest and most powerful military and industrial site in the Proxima System and the most populated moon in the Confederation.

The Twelve Titans

Spartan, Jesus, Teresa, Marcus and a dozen other marines stood on the observation platform on the outer ring of the section. This section was separate to the rotating ring by a short shaft and airlock to the rest of the ship. The windows were small and polarised in case of flares but the view was still incredible. Along the one side were several chairs and even a small table, it was almost civilised. On the wall was a picture of the Santa Maria from her early days as a colony ship. There was a large hydroponic section towards the sterns that Spartan didn't ever recall seeing on the current ship. It must have been removed to make way for more fuel or storage. From their slowly rotating position they had a panoramic view of the Fleet and it was a sight to behold. The view gave them three rotations a minute and at that speed they needed to concentrate on one thing at a time. It was easy to feel sick, even in space.

The Santa Maria had been their home for some time that they had almost forgotten what anything else looked like. Unlike their own ship, they were now surrounded by ships originally built as weapons of war and the difference in their looks was marked. Unlike converted ships, the true warships were built with their fragile crew and fuel sections heavily armoured and protected. The other massive difference was use of space. On a military ship there was no space for luxuries and anywhere that had more than was required could be used for storage, extra armour or simply removed. Without the practicalities of looks of a commercial ship, the warships looked rough and almost insect like from the outside. Extra mounts, gantries and modifications were present on all of them and the older the ship usually the more modifications and changes had taken place. They all carried the symbol of the Interstellar Navy on their bows and each vessel was marked with its vessel code and name. Also present was the massive number of antennae that seemed to protrude from every single side of the ships. Communication was critical in space and no expense spared on the electronics and jamming equipment.

Another key feature of the warships was their obsession with multiband radar systems. In space, it was necessary to monitor for objects of all sizes. At high speed an object the size of a melon could tear great holes through even a battleship. The quicker the Captain knew of danger, the quicker he could avoid it or turn the Point Defence System (PDS) against the threat. The PDS was part of every military ship and now many of the civilian vessels. It comprised a multiband radar installation and a series of low-tech kinetic weapon turrets. These were essentially modern versions of the machine guns and automatic cannons of the twentieth century. In space, they fired a cloud of solid shot in the direction of a threat and had a modest chance of destroying or damaging the target. They were cheap, reasonably effective and a requirement on any vessel travelling the troubles trade lanes of the Proxima Centauri System.

Normally they could just see a small number of the tiny escort cutters that circled all transports that travelled through the Confederation. Transports were vulnerable as they had minimal weapons and armour and carried large numbers of crew and marines. This made them very desirable targets. The cutters were always on the lookout for the small and hard to spot craft that could threaten so many lives. Times had changed and the view today was very different, it almost had the look of an epic painting from the Great War.

There hadn't been much time but the Confederation had managed to assemble seventeen vessels including the Battlecruiser CCS Crusader, the escort carrier Wasp with her complement of eight heavily armed gunboats and shuttles, four cruisers and six marine transports that included their own Santa Maria. The Wasp was due for retirement and had been built to use in the war but arrived just a few months too late. Though she had seen long service, she had never been involved in any major action.

It wasn't the most powerful fleet the System had ever seen but it certainly had access to substantial firepower and had the capacity to conduct a great variety of space and ground based operations. The group of six marine transports had taken on extra troops en route. They now had of over nine hundred marines per vessel, as well as a small number of elite Special Forces commandos, the best marines in the entire military. Each of the marine transports was a mirror of the Santa Maria, but they all had peculiarities in their engines and basic internal layout. On board, they carried the usual mixture of unarmoured shuttles, assault landing craft and heavily armoured troop transports. The landing craft were small but optimised for high-speed combat operations, whereas the transports were able to carry company-sized units directly into the fight. More vessels were on the way from Alpha Centauri and if they waited they could add another two battleships and an extra two-dozen warships. But it would be months before they arrived with the journey time of over three hundred days. Confed had demanded immediate action to retake the transit stations and Titan Naval Station. The marines had been given no more information, as the battle plan was being kept secret and known only to the senior commanders in the Fleet.

"What do you think the plan is?"

Spartan sighed, as he watched the ships moving outside.

"I doubt it will be anything fancy, Marcus. The Fleet has been assembled fast and we're already on our way aren't we? What worries me is that it doesn't take a genius to work out that if you take something that belongs to somebody else they are gonna want it back. We can pussy foot about but I doubt they are stupid. No matter the plan they will be ready and this is gonna get messy, fast."

"Wow, you're a real optimist today you know that. I heard from one of the ensigns that we changed course nearly two days ago but he wouldn't say to where. It looks like the Fleet is going somewhere, the question is where?" asked Teresa.

"Hmm, let me think, Titan Naval Station maybe?" said Jesus sarcastically.

The group stood in silence for a moment but Spartan was unusually quiet. He was staring out at the ships in the Fleet.

"What's wrong?"

"Teresa, I just can't believe that an underground movement that has been able to hold off an entire division of infantry on Proxima and then has taken over the orbital bases and stations, is going to be a push over. They obviously have a plan and I doubt it is to sit and wait for us."

"From what I've seen on the news they're blockading Prime and starving the cities and the military of aid. It's not easy to tell exactly what's happening, they're stopping most broadcasts from the surface so we're only getting part of the story," Jesus added.

"What I don't get though is why they even need external aid or support? They're a goddamned planet, surely than can just carry on with or without anything else coming in," Marcus said.

Corporal Williams, one of the marines from third

platoon was nearby and heard the discussion. He called over to them.

"I know three guys that are in frontline down at the Bone Mill. The last I heard from them is that the Zealots have attacked a lot of the transport and are destroying or taking over much of the storage and production facilities. It isn't far off a civil war down there and yet they are still fighting in that shit hole of a pit."

"I didn't know it had gone so quickly. How have they been able to turn things against us so fast?" asked Teresa, genuinely concerned.

Williams wandered over, checking over his shoulder when he reached them. "This goes nowhere else now, right?"

They all moved closer, keen to hear whatever gossip he'd uncovered.

"From what I've heard the trouble on Prime was an inside job. The Zealots have got support right up to the top, my source said it goes right to the Council!"

"Bullshit!"

"Shut the fuck up, man, I said to keep this to yourself. Look, Marcus, believe me or not, you have to admit it is pretty crazy that a bunch of religious fanatics have gone from blowing up the odd transport to a full military takeover of stations, cities and warships in just a few months. You know they have at least one battleship guarding Titan Naval Station, right? What if they've got more?"

"What if they turn the guns onto the Station?" Spartan asked.

"Yeah, man, you're right. If they do that what can we do? We send in a hundred marines and they destroy the place. Whatever they're planning it had better be good," said Jesus.

In the Combat Information Centre (CIC) the senior commanders of the Fleet were assembled. The room was circular in shape and they were stood around a large table on which a three dimensional model of the Proxima System was displayed. At this distance, it showed all the planets and collections of moons and satellites. The first thing that was obvious was that Prime and her number of stations was the most significant part of the sector. Kerberos was a close second and that planet featured over a dozen inhabited moons and mining stations. There were certainly plenty of other planets and moons but none the equal of the jewel of the Confederation, Prime. In the corner the Admiral stood as a veritable army of intelligence chiefs, ships' captains and marine commanders crowded in. The Admiral walked to the centre of the room, flanked by her two marine bodyguards.

"Good evening, I will keep this brief as we'll have much preparation to do. We are seventeen hours from Proxima Prime and the situation remains fluid on both the transit stations, Titan Naval Station and on the planet's surface.

Before we go over the details of the plan we will examine the latest intelligence." She signalled to Anderson.

"In the last twenty-four hours we have managed to get three vessels close enough to scan the area around Prime. What we have found is quite frankly shocking. All of the transit stations are either under enemy control or have been destroyed." He paused for a moment as a murmur of surprise followed this news.

"Three of the stations, Titan's 3, 4, and 10 were destroyed in a mixture of sabotage and suicide attacks. Casualty estimates from the three stations are in excess of two hundred thousand people. The cruiser Acropolis has been crippled and there is currently a major action on board. We assume the crew are attempting to fight off attempts to board her but for now she is dead in space. As for the Proxima System, the rest of the planets are stable and, though there have been some disturbances on some of the moons and stations, we have been able to calm things down. Out here in the Rim things are a little wild, but they always are and this is something we will deal with later."

He pressed a button and the three dimensional model zoomed out to show the Confederation Systems. With a move of his hand, the model zoomed out further to show a series of star systems, a number of light years away.

"Due to the obvious communication delays we have no news on the new colonies at Epsilon Eridani, Gliese 876 or Procyon. We have sent detailed information to them but it will not get there in time to help us nor could they send help even if they wanted to. We can only hope that they have not experienced the same devastation that we have."

With another movement, he brought the star system of Alpha Centauri into view. Its two stars and scores of planets were a rich source of mineral to the Confederation as well as supporting most of the colony worlds and moons.

"We have received word from the forty-two colonies at Alpha Centauri that so far nothing untoward has happened. Military forces have been put on alert and it looks like we might be able to contain this to Prime and the stations. A fleet is being assembled and the 3rd and 4th Marine Regiments have been reactivated in case this goes any further. If, and this is a big if, we can contain this problem, we should be able to stop it right here. If for any reason the revolt spreads outside of Prime a general call to all reservists will go out and the Confederation will be placed on a war footing. Finally, Sol. As with our other distant colonies, we cannot get word to them anytime soon and have sent the same data packets as we sent to Procyon. In short, this immediate situation concerns the colonies in Proxima Centauri. These are all in range of both our forces and the insurgency."

He pressed a few more keys and the map returned to

the planets and its moons.

"Now, current figures show nine stations are occupied. The estimate for occupying forces is around fifty to a hundred insurgents per transit station, with at least five hundred clustered around the naval facilities and habitation zones at Titan Naval Station. This means a lowest estimate of around fifteen hundred of them on the stations alone. From this number we can see the movement must have inside support, they cannot have transported this many people without us noticing, that's what Military Intelligence say anyway," he said seriously.

With another sweep of his hand, the display zoomed down to the surface of the planet. "As for Prime we have a problem. Most communications to and from the planet have been blocked. The Acropolis was trying to collect data via direct data streams when she was hit by three suicide attacks from captured vessels. They were able to send us a large volume of encrypted data before being cut off. From what they sent we know that a large uprising has started in most of the smaller towns and agricultural areas. So far, the cities are under Confed control but there are reports of heavy fighting at the power plants, transport hubs and ports. All operations at the Bone Mill have been halted until the situation is resolved. For now those units are being redeployed to where they are needed most. Elements of the 7th and 12th Regiments are holding the area in case the insurgents try to take advantage of the situation," he said finally.

As he stepped backed a man in a dark, flowing uniform devoid of any insignia, replaced him.

"I represent the logistical service on Prime and have details on the weapons and equipment that has been confirmed as used in the field."

Though most there were not familiar with his garb the more experienced of the officers knew immediately he was from one of the Special Forces intelligence units on the planet.

"Firstly, the Zealots are fighting in much larger numbers than any of our estimates have shown. They are more ruthless than ever before. Even when attacking the primary polar power plant on Prime, they continued until all of them were killed. They attacked with eighty members and did not stop. They are well motivated and our estimates place their planet-side strength anywhere between four and twenty thousand. This figure does not include the unknown number at the Bone Mill. I don't want to confirm or deny this, but there are estimates by field agents that enemy numbers could be five times this number," he said calmly.

The mood in the room was electric. What had been expected to be a thousand people in total was turning into a full scale uprising of kind not seen since the Great War.

"Now, weapons, equipment and tactics. It is clear that the Zealots have been massing supplies and equipment for years. To date, we have come across everything from knives to military issue shotguns and rifles. They are using body armour, most of which is home produced and not effective against our L48 rifles. They are vastly more experienced in hand-to-hand combat and in every engagement where they have been close enough to use edged weapons they have overwhelmed our forces. They are competent with knives, maces and even swords. Some of their close quarter weapon designs are completely new to us. We have reports that these devices are quite capable of punching through the chest armour of a marine," he added, followed by a long pause.

"Finally, vehicles. We have seen evidence of homegrown vehicles, mainly land based and a few aircraft in the north. In general, they seem to prefer ground combat but are capable of hijacking or capturing craft of all kinds. They have the knowledge and skills to repair, modify and operate everything from trains to warships. This suggests knowledge from within our existing security structures," he said before stepping back.

"Before General Rivers explains our plans I would like a full update on the Fleet. Please keep this short as time is critical!" The Admiral ordered.

* * *

Lieutenant Erdeniz lay in his hospital bed gazing out of

the windows. He knew they weren't real, but the view was a direct feed from outside and it was good to see something other than the white walls of the room. He had only recently woken up and the drugs were still swirling inside his body, making him feel as though he had been drinking for the last twenty-four hours. As he lay there the door opened and in walked a captain, flanked by a guard. He marched up to the side of the bed and removed his hat.

"How are you feeling, son?" he asked.

Erdeniz tried to focus on the man but the drugs dulled his senses and it took a few seconds for him to be able to properly focus.

"Uh, um, I'm feeling much better, Sir," he said with much effort.

"Good man. I can't stay long, we're waiting for information on the plan to come through from CIC. I was asked by the Admiral to tell you that she is very grateful for what you did."

"I, I don't understand," came the weak reply.

"When you were attacked it was an attempt by the Zealots to take over the ship. Two of them tried to break into the Admiral's quarters when you triggered the alarm. Over a dozen officers were already dead when you set it off. Another twenty seconds and the entire command staff would have gone too. You have our thanks, you have literally saved this crew and this vessel," he said with a smile.

Erdeniz was still confused and didn't fully understand what the man was saying but at least it didn't sound like he'd done something bad.

"Now, get a little rest, I will send somebody along later to check on you. Good job!"

Returning his hat to his head he exited the room smartly and closed the door behind him.

* * *

General Rivers approached the waiting marines in the main hall of the Santa Maria.

"As Commander of the 6th Marine Regiment I have been given command of the ground element of the operation to retake control of all the stations around Prime."

On the screen in front of the assembled marines he brought up the massive Titan Naval Station that was built into the largest of Prime's moons.

"As you can see, the Station is well guarded by the Battleship Victorious and the crippled Resolution. We cannot even consider an operation to take the Station until these vessels have been eliminated."

Hitting a button the image changed to an aerial view of the plan.

"The Fleet will split into three squadrons, the first two will move in and take control of the eight transit stations and hopefully draw some of the vessels away from Titan Naval Yard. Each of these stations is small, some are simple docks and shipyards, others are used to move civilian traffic. We need to take them all back and fast. By hitting them simultaneously, the enemy will not be able to reinforce each other. A single group will then move in to engage the battleship as the commando unit heads to the naval yard eliminating the main guns. Once the primary defences are down we will move in and launch a coordinated assault on the Station itself. This is where you come in." He pointed to the assembled men and women.

"If we cannot stop this warship the entire operation will be called off. I cannot stress to you how important it is that we succeed. We have the best ships for this part of the mission and I have no doubt we will be successful. The real crux of the operation will rest on the regiment's task of capturing Titan Naval Station. The Station is operating at one quarter normal gravity and looks like the toughest assignment I have seen in my years in the marines."

"This unit has been tasked with the most dangerous mission of all and I will not hide from you the difficulties you face. I will say that it is a testament to your training and skill that this ship has been chosen to lead the attack. As the rest of the Fleet engages the enemy, you will spearhead an overwhelming assault on the Station itself. Each platoon has specific objectives including securing the dock and shipyards. Those who have completed the commando training will join the team that will move into the command areas and secure the guns prior to the arrival of the marine transports. The main assault cannot go ahead until the guns are silenced. Small landing craft are fast enough to hopefully make it but our larger transports will be turned to dust before they reach five kilometres from their objectives."

The officer turned to the marines, noting their eagerness to get stuck in.

"I know your training has been cut short but from the reports I've seen you are in the best shape we could hope for. You are fit, equipped and ready to do your job. Under normal circumstances we would wait but this situation is spiralling out of control. We have support from the gunboats of Wasp and this should be enough to provide adequate cover to get inside. Your squad leaders have their specific plans, please get a few hours rest, contact your loved ones, do whatever you damned please just be in the shuttle bays and ready for combat operation in four hours. Good luck, marines!"

As the marines were dismissed, Spartan and his group moved to the side of the area. Have you checked the boards? Which group are we going in with?" he asked.

"No idea, come on, let's find out!" Teresa said as she ran off to the end of the hall where a large screen showed the roster and the combat teams. There were dozens of them, each assigned certain equipment and shuttles for their missions.

"Yeah, here we are!" shouted Jesus.

"What is this?" Marcus looked less than impressed.

Spartan stepped in closer, reading the board. Next to their names and half of their platoon was the assignment to the Commando Support Group.

"Support Group? What kind of gay shit is this?"

"You can be such an idiot, Marcus!" Teresa was reading the board.

"Teresa is right, Marcus, the CSG is part of the Commando Team that is going for the hostages. The support group's job is to provide fire support and assistance as required. This is the highest you can get on your first mission," said Spartan.

"We'd better go and get ready then, we need to meet the Commando Team and go over the mission before we board."

"Yeah," added Jesus as he made his way to his quarters.

Spartan turned to head off but Teresa grabbed his shoulder, turning him back around. "How long do we have?" she asked placing a special emphasis on the word 'we'.

Spartan looked up at the clock and back at her. "I think we can manage thirty minutes."

"Thirty minutes, hmm," she said with a grin. "Yeah, I think that will work!"

Pulling his arm Teresa dragged Spartan off down the

corridor and towards her quarters, much to the amusement of the rest of the squad.

* * *

Over half of the Fleet had already moved off leaving the battlecruiser CCS Crusader, the Santa Maria and a small number of cruisers, destroyers and gunboats in reserve. This strike force was the main force designated for the attack on Titan Naval Station and though it looked formidable to Admiral Jarvis it was a fraction of what she wanted for such a risky operation. Along the gun decks of the warship the gun ports were all open and the weapon system of each ship was ready for action.

In the Combat Information Centre of the CCS Crusader, General Rivers and Admiral Jarvis poured over the latest report on the operation. Most of the officers had now gone and there were less than a dozen people in the room, all of which were working through screens of information and managing the large collection of vessels.

Lieutenant Nilsson, a dark brown haired officer with distinctive, green-flecked brown eyes turned from her communications desk.

"Admiral, I'm receiving urgent messages from Titan Naval Station, the insurgents are calling for assistance from their comrades. Shall I jam their communications?"

"Negative, we need to split them off as much as we

can, let the message through."

The Lieutenant turned back to her display and continued to monitor communication between the ships. On the main three-dimensional tactical map the Admiral followed the open stages of the operation. They were only four hours in and the first wave were in battle around half of the small stations.

"Reports from Bunker Hill say that all five transports have started their ground assault. So far they have taken thirty-seven casualties and now have control of two stations. Resistance is stronger than expected but they are making solid progress. Captain Jones estimates around three hours to capture the remainder of the stations."

"Good, that is a very good start," replied the Admiral. She turned and looked at the tactical display, watching the movement of the vessels in orbit.

"Any news on Titan Naval Station, any movement?"

Lieutenant Nilsson connected to her opposite numbers on the other vessels, quickly collating data. "Negative, no movement on the vessels guarding the Station."

"As expected, they are waiting for our main strike." The Admiral picked up the intercom. "Captain Matthias, are your ships ready?"

"Affirmative, Ajax, Hector and Achilles are in position and weapons batteries are charged and ready."

"Good work, Captain, send in your cruiser wing to Titan Naval Station immediately, we need to let them think this is the main attack. Pray to the gods that they take the bait and engage your forces. Do not leave the area until you have taken fire. I know this is a big request but I need you to take enough fire to warrant a withdrawal, make it look good, Captain."

There was a brief pause before the Captain of the cruiser group returned.

"Understood, Admiral, we will put on a good show. We won't leave the area until they think they are winning."

"God speed, Captain," said the Admiral replacing the intercom. General Rivers turned to her.

"If they are ready when we jump in we'll face their full numbers before we can bring our guns to bear. We need to be patient, every minute we can add to their return trip will give us just that bit of extra time to deal with Victorious."

"I understand, General, and I am aware of the difficulty your troops are facing on the stations. We will move in as soon as I am confident we have a chance of breaking through."

The massive battlecruiser rumbled and a series of vibrations rattled through the warship. General Rivers turned to Lieutenant Nilsson who was evidently concerned.

"It's the forward gun batteries, they are charging up their capacitors prior to battle. We can't charge up all the batteries at once, not even on this ship," he said with a stern grin.

The Admiral moved past the General, facing the

communications officer.

"Lieutenant Nilsson, can you put me on the battlegroup's intercom, it is speech time," she said with as much humour as she could muster in such a serious situation.

"This is Admiral Jarvis. Approximately one hour ago elements of our task force began the first stages in the operation to retake the transit stations orbiting Proxima Prime. Our battlegroup, spearheaded by Crusader, will start our attack in less than ninety minutes. All medical teams are to report to their sections, marines will prepare to repel boarders and all gunners please check and recheck your weapons. This will be the first capital ship engagement since the Great War and if it is anything like historic encounters, we can expect heavy damage and casualties on both sides. Admiral Jarvis, out."

She replaced the intercom and turned back to the tactical map. The display showed two-dozen vessels in position near the outer ring of stations around the planet. Several faster colours indicated the gunboats from the carrier Wasp. It was their job to provide cover from any potential attacks by smaller vessels. She turned back to the General.

"If for any reason we are unable to regain control of the Station I have been given full authorisation to neutralise Titan Naval Station and every soul on it. Her face showed that this wasn't an option she really wanted to consider.

"Destroy the Station, do we even have the firepower to

do that?"

"I have asked our engineers to run simulations and all they can tell me is that if we can mass all of our firepower on the Station we can render it useless after about sixty minutes of continuous bombardment. We can't do anything more than make it unsuitable for life, General."

"Perhaps if I could get commandos onto the Station they could place a number of thermite plasma charges at key locations and do the same job. It won't be pretty, Admiral, but if the Crusader is busy we might not have the luxury of turning all the guns on the Station. What about the hostages?"

"We are to rescue them of course, unless this puts the Fleet in a position whereby we cannot end this revolt. Either way the capture of Titan Naval Station will be resolved, one way or the other," she said as she turned back to the displays.

* * *

Spartan and Teresa were both laid out and relaxed. Spartan held a bottle of water in one hand as Teresa sat looking out of the projection window at the Fleet. With their gun ports open the ships looked much rougher than normal, it was a sight she had not seen before. Between the capital ships the gunboats and shuttles moved back and forth, ferrying people and weapons prior to the battle. The

Crusader was a sight to behold and she couldn't imagine any vessel being able to stand up to her bulk. She was mesmerised by the rotating bands that ran the length of the ship, each one bristling with open ports and slowing the ship to fire in any direction from above or below or front port or stern. The weakest section in terms of firepower was the bow and stern where the warship was fitted with just a single weapon battery, much like a bow chaser on an old-fashioned tall ship.

"How can any ship stop the Crusader? Just look at her, Spartan," she said as she stared at the majestic shape of the battlecruiser.

Spartan rolled over, looking out at the massive warship.

"She is impressive but from what I've been reading so is the Victorious. That old warship was actually involved in the Great War. She is responsible for the crippling of two other battleships and even survived a ramming by a cruiser. All of the advantages of the Crusader are going to be wasted in this battle. She has lighter armour, the same weapons and the only real improvement is the better engines. On paper I'd give the edge to Victorious," he said with a hint of regret.

"You're assuming that they even know how to operate the ship or have enough crew to man her."

"True, but you're also assuming that none of the crew had a hand in the takeover to start with. If that's so then we could be about to attack an experienced and prepared battleship," he said as he sat up and rubbed his eyes. "I just hope the Intel guys have done their homework," he sighed.

The two pulled on their fatigues in silence as they considered the current operation and the part they had yet to play. Their clothes were scattered around the berth and it took them a few minutes to get ready. Teresa moved closely to Spartan, looking carefully at his face.

"Don't do anything stupid now, I would like to see you come back," she said with a smile.

"No problem, I have absolutely no intention of letting some religious crazy get in my way, you just watch yourself. We have unfinished business!" he said as he swung himself out of the room and into the corridor.

It didn't take long and they were soon moving down the main corridor where scores of other marines were collecting their gear and boarding their craft. Marcus and Jesus along with another eight marines were waiting in a group at the far right, separate to the rest of them. Spartan and Teresa moved over. Most of them were wearing their full PDS gear and the rest were in the process of fitting on their armour and checking their weapons for the hundredth time.

"We're supposed to wait here for Colonel West. He's leading the commando operation. You ever met the guy?" asked Marcus.

"Nope, never heard of him," answered Teresa.

"You have now," said a short, scrawny looking man who appeared behind Spartan.

The man stood with a group of a dozen similar looking men and one woman. Though they wore normal Personal Defence Suits, they had a slightly different camouflage pattern to the rest of the marines and their equipment was certainly older and well used. The officer stepped forward and shook each of their hands.

"This is my team, I take it you've gone over the mission briefing. Normally we wouldn't take newbies on a first mission but our numbers are small and we need every man we can get. We will go in first, you'll provide backup and a tactical reserve. This doesn't mean you'll be sitting back in the shuttles, you are just as important as the rest of the unit. Stay together and keep an eye on the guy next to you." He looked around the group of fresh marines.

The tannoy system blared loudly across the ship.

"All units to your posts, we are loading the shuttles. I repeat, all to their station, it is not a drill!" came the order and it was repeated over and over.

"Let's go!" The Colonel shouted as his team moved down the shaft and towards the waiting shuttles.

As they moved off Spartan lifted his hand and smacked his hand onto Teresa's outstretched palm.

"Good luck!" she said.

CHAPTER SEVEN

Though not the most famous, the CCS Invincible was a ship with a history that was unique to any other vessel in the Fleet. During the Great War she was the last battleship to engage another battleship in open battle. Most engagements were fought by carriers and cruisers, but by a chance encounter she had run into the rebel warship, the Redoubtable. This battle between two equals has been studied for generations, as to the power and the futility of putting two such behemoths against each other.

After more than twenty hours of continuous battle and over twelve thousand casualties there was still no victor. Both vessels were quickly disabled and unable to leave the area and neither captain would surrender his vessel. It wasn't until the arrival of the fourteen ships of the Kerberos Squadron that the battle could be decided. Five of those ships were also lost until the

Redoubtable was finally destroyed.

The shattered but still operational hulk of the CCS Invincible and the remnants of the Kerberos Squadron were present at the signing of the armistice. The old ship is a relic of the Great War and is still moored at the Fleet Headquarters in Alpha Centauri. A visit to the ship is part of the required training for all naval cadets.

Ships of the Interstellar Navy

In the Combat Information Centre of the CCS Crusader it was decision time and the Admiral and her staff were getting nervous. As every minute passed the chances of a decisive and relatively bloodless conclusion slipped away. From inside the bustling room a dozen officers moved back and forth, updating the tactical display and co-ordinating actions between the numerous ships involved in the battle. Hundreds of officers both on the ground and aboard the myriad of vessels involved in the operation did their best to keep everything moving smoothly.

The ground assault on the smaller manmade stations had now been raging for over two hours and there were no signs that the rest of the transit stations would be falling anytime soon. Though much smaller than the massive Titan Naval Station, each was the home to hundreds or thousands of people and couldn't be simply destroyed from orbit. The stations circled the planet of Prime at different altitudes with the most remote being hundreds of kilometres from the planet. They offered a variety of landing platforms, refineries, ports and shipyards for Prime. Though Titan Naval Station was massive, most of the inhabited areas were situated on the nearside of the moon that faced Prime. The bulk of the population was clustered around the civilian port and naval yard.

As expected, resistance had been heavy but the arrival of volunteer fighters from the planet had not been spotted. On several of the stations there were hundreds of additional fighters and though their skills were limited, they were easily able to hold off and keep the attacking marines busy. These last minute volunteers showed no regard for human life and they were happy to be used as human bombs or simply to draw the marines' fire to expose their positions to the more experienced Zealot fighters. The latest reports put the attacking marines' casualties now at over a hundred and as each minute went by more figures came in. The only black mark so far was that one shuttle with eighty-two civilians and twelve marines had been lost due to a suicide bomber making her way inside. The craft had almost reached the transport when her vest detonated. At least the shuttle hadn't made it inside the transport or it could have easily caused many more casualties. The one piece of good news was that over eight hundred civilians had been rescued by the operations on the smaller Titan stations and were already being shipped by shuttlecraft to the waiting ships. It was bloody work but they appeared to be making progress.

Of even more of a serious concern to the Admiral, was that the cruiser wing had just moved into range of the Naval Station. This was a risky gambit as the battleship had lots of options available and the last thing she wanted was to have to slug it out with an almost impregnable vessel right next to the Station. If they could get her to move the assault would have been pulled off. She prayed the defenders would take the bait. On the tactical screen she watched the line of three cruisers moving in formation to the Station. The three cruisers were powerful ships and easily capable of taking on several similar sized vessels or even one of the stations on their own. A ship like the Victorious however was another matter. The only people capable of producing a vessel of that size and power were the shipyards and engineers of the Confederation Navy. She didn't enjoy the irony of having to face a ship that had been built and designed to be almost impregnable for the very people that would now have to attack it.

"Captain Matthias, give me a sitrep," she ordered.

"Affirmative, Admiral. We are twelve kilometres from the Station and so far have been ignored. There is massive electronic and radar jamming in the area and we are having a hard time scanning for power signatures and weapons. We can see their disposition though and it looked like we might be in luck," he said.

General Rivers moved closer, examining the tactical display and then looked back at the Admiral.

"I don't like it," he said.

"Understood, Captain, take your ships in, just don't get too close that you can't leave. We are twelve minutes behind you. Good luck," she added.

"Thank you, Admiral, out," he said and the intercom went silent.

* * *

On the deck of the cruiser CCS Achilles, Captain Matthias watched the massive Titan Naval Station through the glass. At first glance it looked just like a moon, but on closer examination the huge jetties, gantries and cranes could be found on almost every section of the surface. Around the orbit of the moon were large numbers of ships though most were small freighters and transports. What he was more interested in were the two warships the heavy cruiser CCS Resolution and the battleship CCS Victorious. The first ship was still venting gasses. It looked like it had sustained heavy damage. Victorious however appeared completely unscathed.

"Engineering, I need everything you have on the warships, stat!" he shouted to the three officers on his right. The men were sitting in front of a large display that presented masses of data on both the cruiser wing and the enemy vessels.

The three cruisers were vessels of the Achilles class and had been in service for over forty years. Each carried thick armour down the flanks and batteries of railguns in sections along their lengths. They were also equipped with over a hundred point defence weapons designed to protect against torpedoes and missile impacts as well as to defend against small ships, boarding pods and landing craft.

"Sir, it appears both vessels are powered up and ready," said the first man.

"Ready?" said the Captain to himself.

"Wait, I have movement on the Victorious, yes, she's moving out of her berth," he said excitedly.

Captain Matthias grabbed the intercom to inform the Fleet of the good news.

"Admiral, Admiral?" he asked, but there was no response.

"Captain, our communications are being jammed this close to the Station. We need to withdraw from their electronic counter measures range," explained the second officer.

"No, we need to buy the Fleet time, we have to get the ship as far from the Station as possible. If we fight at this distance the marine landing craft won't get within ten kilometres of the Station. Have you seen the point defence grid on that thing? She could wipe out every shuttle and boarding party we send in minutes," he said.

The Captain moved back to the forward window of the bridge where he had a good view of the Station and the enemy. It was a dangerous mission but one he was sure his wing could achieve. He turned and gave the order.

"It's time, send them in."

He nodded and quickly pulled down the intercom and called over to the communications officers.

"Put me on a secure ship-to-ship channel with Ajax and Hector," he said. The officer connected the vessels in seconds.

"Follow attack plan Charlie, maintain distance and engage Victorious. It is imperative that we keep clear of her broadsides. Stay at range and if possible aim for her engines, God speed to you all."

In seconds, the three massive cruisers fired up their engines and moved into a column as they manoeuvred into position to orbit the battleship. Unlike the heavier ships, the cruisers were designed for much higher speeds and their manoeuvrability and acceleration was impressive. Within moments, the bright glow from their engines propelled them forwards and into action.

The vessels were huge but still only one quarter the size of the Victorious. Normally they would be commanding small patrols and even fleets but hunting down capital ships was a job for a mixed force that would include carriers, cruisers and gunboats.

As the three fast moving cruisers adjusted their course, a series of bright flashes along the bow of the old battleship indicated the start of the battle. The battleship was easily double the width of the cruisers and its heavy armoured prow hit batteries of weapon ports. From such a close range the first volley hit almost instantly, the solid projectiles tearing through the Achilles, the lead ship of the cruiser wing. As the heavy metal projectiles struck the starboard flank of the ship it rocked from the impact. Each shell was the size of a man and tore huge chunks from the side. A lesser ship would have been cut in half, but the thick, multi-layered armour plating absorbed at least some of the initial attack.

"Jesus!" Captain Matthias shouted as he saw a large number of red lights flashing on his displays.

Throughout the room the displays were flashing with all kinds of critical data. From his view on the bridge he could see great chunks of the ship torn off and drifting into space. A crack appeared in the glass and without even checking with the crew, the computer system brought down the blast shutters to prevent any chance of as breach.

"Damage report!" he barked.

Lieutenant Jones, the senior engineer, was stunned by the damage he could see on his screen and it took him a few seconds to compose himself.

"Sir, we've taken four hits to the lower weapons decks. I have breaches and decompression in twelve compartments, twenty-seven casualties already reported, more coming in. One battery is out of action."

"Tactical!" shouted the Captain.

"Sir, in this position she is currently only able to bring her forward guns to bear. If we cross her T we can maximise our firepower and reduced potential damage," said Lieutenant LeMarche.

"Why are they coming straight at us? If they simply presented their broadside they could fight us off with just a few volleys?" he shouted.

"Sir, You are assuming they have a competent crew, what if they can barely control the ship? It would explain their direct line attack and exposing their bow. If they keep going like this there is a chance we could cripple her."

"A cruiser wing defeating a battleship, now that would be a first." The Captain said to himself as he smiled.

As he considered the battle, another volley of smaller calibre shells peppered the hull of his cruiser. They were probably the point defence systems being directed to add fire. They were unable to penetrate the thick armour of the Achilles but they did give the Captain hope as to the skill and experience of his opponent.

"Cross their T and put a broadside down their throats!" he shouted the order as he held on firmly to the grab handles as another impact rocked the ship.

The CCS Achilles was the first ship in three formations and as she turned hard to her left she exposed her entire right flank to the approaching battleship. The Ajax and Hector moved into the same position, following the Achilles like a line of elephants holding each other's tails. The formation had its benefits though. Just as the wooden tall ships of old, these modern ships of the line had the greatest number of weapons running along their length. This meant that they could do more damage firing sideways than head on. The current formation allowed all three ships to bring all their guns to bear on the enemy. There were other benefits too. The weapons all the vessels were using were solid shot electric railguns. This ammunition could easily penetrate the deck and afterdeck of even a fully armoured ship. By hitting the enemy from the front, the shot would punch through the bow and run a long way through the vessel. The return fire from the battleship however would only be able to strike the flanks of the cruisers and damage whatever lay between the sides of the ship.

As the Achilles reached an almost perfect ninety-degree angle from the Victorious she opened fire. Each gunport fired in sequence and the entire flank of the cruiser disappeared in a bright blast of venting plasma gas. The wave of heavy projectiles was accelerated out of the gunports and towards the closing enemy vessel. As the torrent of heavy shells slammed into the ancient battleship the other two cruisers added their own volleys. The first counterattack by the three ships sent over fifty heavy projectiles and over half struck exactly where they needed to.

"I'm detecting multiple impacts on their bow and port quarter, substantial damage to their forward guns I think, there's certainly no sign of return fire," said Lieutenant LeMarche.

"Excellent, that is more like it. How long till the next volley?" he asked.

"Thirty seconds, Captain," came the immediate reply. "We could continue the volleys but it will leave us vulnerable while we recharge the main batteries," he explained.

"No, I want our cruiser wing to turn to sequential fire, I want a continuous rain of metal on her, don't give their crew time to think. If what I think is true, they are inexperienced and we need them to make sure they are unable to come up with a suitable plan. Keep poking and prodding them and she'll stay with us," he ordered.

Although a full volley or broadside was massively powerful, it did leave the ship with a full complement of guns that were unloaded and that meant each ship was unable to return fire for a good half a minute. That was enough time to suffer major damage or even loss of a ship. The sequential fire option was simple, each battery fired its weapons in turn so that by the time the last battery fired the first was recharged and ready to fire. From space it looked like each gun was taking it in turn to fire. Though it was much less effective in the short-term, it did mean a vessel could keep up firing on a ship without pausing. This type of fire was generally reserved for fighting against smaller vessels or when fighting multiple opponents, as it gave a higher rate of fire and the option to spit fire quickly and easily. This battle was different though, they needed to annoy the enemy so that they could draw her away from the Station.

As the Achilles' weapon batteries reached their capacity the firing resumed and Captain Matthias watched in satisfaction as shot after shot blasted out into space and against the Victorious who was still moving towards them at ever increasing speed. The other cruisers began firing and the gulf between the four ships filled with the ultra high-speed projectiles. A small number of shells came back from the enemy, but it appeared Lieutenant LeMarche was correct and most of their forward guns were non-functioning and presumably destroyed.

Captain Matthias checked his tactical display noting that his cruiser wing had already moved two kilometres away from the Station and the battleship was still following. It was bloody work but it appeared the plan was working.

"Sir, if we don't change course the Victorious will be on us in less than sixty seconds," said Lieutenant LeMarche.

The Captain double-checked his screens before turning over to engineering.

"What is her status?" he barked.

"Sir, based on the number of guns inoperative on

the front port and bow section I would suggest we have removed a quarter of her guns. She does have dorsal weapon batteries but they are not firing either. Maybe they do not have a full crew or her systems are not all working?" he replied.

"Interesting, we might have a chance here," said LeMarche. "We could turn and draw her away. If we do that, we complete our objectives for the Fleet and the mission. We risk less but she could simply turn back. If we stand and return to volley fire we could cripple her and remove her from the fight completely," he added.

As the gunfire continued and the ship rocked from the high-energy weapons the Captain considered the possibilities.

"I say we take the middle road. We fight for a little longer and see if we can cripple or slow her down enough to give us options. I see this as a golden opportunity. One way or another, Victorious will have to be dealt with. If not by us, then maybe one of our marine transports will have to contend with her guns. I will not have that. At the very least, we can hurt her before we leave. Reload the guns and resume volley fire. I think we have her attention now. It is about time we really hurt her!" he growled.

"Captain," he nodded and began relaying the orders to the ships.

Captain Matthias turned back to his communications officer.

"Have you been able to make contact with the Admiral yet?" he asked.

"No, Captain, we are still too close to the Station."

"How much further?" he demanded.

At this speed, another ten to eleven minutes, Sir," he explained before turning back to the display.

A series of lights flashed across the bridge and panic set in with the engineering officers and tactical.

"Captain, we've got a problem!" cried Lieutenant LeMarche. "She's accelerating towards Ajax!"

The mighty battleship was now only a short distance from the three cruisers and had altered course slightly towards the middle ship, Ajax. Volley fire from the cruisers now pounded her hull.

"Captain, my scans show her prow has been badly damaged though most of her weapon systems appear undamaged. She is far less damaged than our results suggested. Either she is unwilling or unable to use them. Wait, I'm detecting a power surge, she is running at over 120 per cent charge, she is going to fire a double broadside," he added.

"Dear God!" shouted LeMarche, as he realised the battleship was about to unleash every weapon it carried. "They are not damaged, Captain. Instead of firing she's been slowly topping up her weapon banks so she can fire both sides at once. There is a chance the surge could destroy her and us with her!" he shouted.

"A suicide attack? Are you sure? That old ship could easily fire a few doubles before taking damage!"

The communications officer tried to reach the other two cruisers to warn them to move to full power but it was too late. The battleship steamed through the three kilometre wide gap between Hector and Ajax, her right hull facing Ajax and her left Hector. Time seemed to slow as the officers watched in horror as the battleship positioned herself perfectly to attack two ships at the same time. There was a terrible flash as both of her flanks were covered in venting plasma. Every single weapon that still worked opened fire. Hundred of rounds smashed through the bow and bridge of the Hector. At least four entered the command centre, instantly killing the captain and his officers. The rest of the shots ploughed through the entire length of the ship, tearing through section after section. In less than thirty seconds the ship was left a burning hulk with hundreds of crew already rushing for the lifeboats. She was of no use to anybody anymore.

The Ajax fared only slightly better as her engines absorbed most of the weapons' fire. The overwhelming barrage of metal tore the engines and fuel storage tanks apart, instantly leaving the vessel with nothing more than manoeuvring thrusters. Some of the rounds penetrated as far as the port batteries and set off a chain of explosions through the length of the ship. The fires were serious but the ship was still able to move and incredibly returned fire with a number of the surviving weapon batteries.

On board the Achilles Captain Matthias was stunned. In just seconds his wing had been reduced to only one functioning ship, one heavily damaged and one crippled. The Victorious was already slowing down and turning around to bring her alongside the damaged Ajax.

"Sir, we have only two decisions, either we turn and give assistance to Ajax or we go full burn, save the ship and warn the Fleet," LeMarche said.

Captain Matthias said nothing; his attention focussed on the crippled Hector. He knew many of the officers and he couldn't believe the damage she had sustained so quickly. As he watched, a bright green flash tore through the centre of the Hector that split the vessel in two.

"My God!" he cried, still unable to comprehend what had happened.

"Sir, we must decide, now!" LeMarche shouted, finally shocking him out of his stupor.

"Captain, I'm through to the Admiral, relaying tactical data now," said the communications officer.

Captain Matthias stood up straight, his expression serious. He turned to LeMarche.

"They know the situation and the Victorious is away from the Station. Turn us around and engage her stern. I want this bastard's engines and I want them now!" he shouted.

LeMarche moved to the tactical display and coordinated the battle between the remaining two ships as the Captain moved to the window, watching the battle in all its terrible glory.

The Ajax, though unable to escape was still quick and in less than twenty seconds her port side was facing the starboard side of the Victorious as the two ships faced off. Both vessels pounded each other with salvo after salvo, both taking damage from the massed batteries of railguns. The Achilles turned hard to her left and once again crossed the T of the mighty battleship. This time though they timed their salvos to hit slightly off centre so that they ran down the flanks of the ship, rather than impacting on the reinforced prow. The damage was impressive but as the debris drifted it was clear that the Victorious could take this kind of fire for hours. Small fires burned at points inside the outer structure but the massive vessel was intact and all of her broadside batteries were operational. As the broadsides continued, it quickly became clear that Ajax couldn't take much more. Half of her guns were out of action and fires were running along her entire length.

"Sir, message from the Ajax, they have breaches in engineering, they are advising us to leave the area," said the Lieutenant.

Captain Matthias swore, angry that he was about to lose his only other vessel and her huge compliment of crew. "Double charge the guns and bring us in close, I want to hit her close and hard!" he barked.

As the warship moved in closer to the battle the three ships disappeared in a cloud of projectiles and plasma gas.

* * *

"We need to move faster!" argued Admiral Jarvis as she watched the tactical display as her group of ships moved in towards the Titan Naval Station. The Fleet had almost completed the trip from where they had been assembled at Kerberos and would reach Prime shortly.

"Any more news on the Achilles? Is she still in the fight?" she asked.

"Unknown, Admiral, just static and interference. Whatever is going on we'll find out in about thirty seconds," answered Lieutenant Andrews, the tactical officer, as the Fleet moved ever closer.

The Fleet, headed by the mighty battlecruiser was heading directly for the Station and the Admiral could only hope that the cruisers had done enough to clear their way in. As they reached within one thousand kilometres their sensors were able to burn through the perimeter and provide some tactical data.

"We're showing the Achilles and the Victorious are still fighting. Achilles is heavily damaged and venting fuel. Ajax is evacuating, Hector is gone. Can't get through to Titan Naval Station yet, no signs of capital ships in the area though," said Andrews.

As the Fleet moved ever closer, the flashes of battle were now visible from most of the ships. News of the loss of the Hector had spread through the rest of the Fleet like wildfire and some were undoubtedly concerned as to the ability of the CCS Crusader to hold off such a well renowned warship. They were already slowing as they reached just fifty kilometres from the Station.

"Admiral, the Victorious is changing course, she is heading our way. Achilles is burning," said Andrews.

"It's time," she said to herself as she signalled to Lieutenant Nilsson to put her on with the Fleet.

"This is Admiral Jarvis. We are at our objective. The Station is clear but we are facing a fully operational Victorious. All group leaders begin your attack, she must be stopped, no matter the cost. Marines are clear to start your landings. Stay close to your escorts, this is going to be rough. I repeat, all offensive actions are authorised. Good luck," she said in a calm voice.

As her orders spread through the Fleet, the bulk of the vessels turned to face the damaged battleship Victorious. Only the Santa Maria and Santa Cruz, with almost two thousand marines on board, and their group of four escort gunboats continued on their trajectory towards the Titan Naval Station. The gunboats were from the deck of the CCS Wasp and carried a dozen men and massive firepower. Today these four craft were configured for point defence. Each one carried additional defensive pods to protect against incoming projectiles and missiles. They pushed out in front of the Santa Maria.

The CCS Crusader, though new, had not been tested in battle before and this was her first opportunity to prove herself against the toughest opponent she could ever expect to face, a CCS battleship.

Spartan and Teresa were sitting towards the rear of their marine landing craft. It was cramped and much smaller than they expected. It carried a full platoon of marines inside its thick armoured structure as well as extra supplies, spare weapons and some heavy equipment. Everything a commando unit could need to establish a beachhead for the rest of the marines.

It was shaped like an angry wasp, its legs stuck up below and its power plants mounted high above the fuselage. Unlike the gunboats it was lightly armed with just defensive weapon mounts fitted around the body, each one designed to be operated by the marines onboard. Spartan and Teresa had been commandeered to control the right-hand door gun though the name was somewhat of a misnomer. The weapon was a twin -barrelled machinegun, an improved version of the same weapon used generations before in the ground wars on Earth. It might be low tech but it was reliable and functioned both on the ground and in the vacuum of space. The combat landing craft were unpressurised so only those in sealed suits could either crew or travel in them. The front of the craft was rounded and massively thick, apparently in tests it could sustain a single impact from a capital ship mounted railgun and against lighter weapons could easily absorb substantial fire over the short time it took to reach ground or ship based targets.

As they moved from the safety of the CCS Santa Maria they travelled past the massive ship from the left side and moved alongside as the rest of the assault craft joined them. As they moved into position, one of the gunboats came nearer, it was easily five times the size of the landing craft and bristled with weapons. Though the craft looked huge it was miniscule in comparison to the Santa Maria which in turn was dwarfed by the size of the battlecruiser CCS Crusader.

From their position they had a clear view of the ongoing battle of the two juggernauts, the Crusader and the Victorious. The two ships were several kilometres apart and bombarding each other with volley after volley. The great bulk, as well as the thick armour of each vessel, precluded any quick victory and as they hammered away at each other the small number of other craft circled around, trying to assist but without drawing too much attention from the wounded warship. After a dozen broadsides the ships looked no further from the end of their battle than when they started.

Slightly off to the right of the two titans the bright flashes continued from the wreck of the Hector at it continued to burn and tear itself apart. Though the ship was destroyed, scores of lifeboats continued to burst out from the damaged sections as the crew desperately tried to avoid the savage inferno of the dying cruiser.

The blazing hulk of Ajax drifted slowly towards the battle but with the damage it must have sustained it was going nowhere fast.

Seated ahead of Teresa and Spartan was the rest of their improvised squad of commandos, waiting for their landing. Each was fully equipped with their sealed suits, weapons and additional equipment. Marcus and Jesus were part of the next squad on the other side of the landing craft and like them, they had been assigned a door gun. Half of the marines were new recruits from the Santa Maria and though they were all keen to get stuck into action, they also looked nervous, really nervous.

The craft shook and the passengers would have rolled to the rear if it weren't for the sturdy straps that kept each of them firmly in their positions. Another reason for the heavy-duty harnesses was that they kept the marines secure when travelling in gravity free space. Contrary to what a few of the recruits had thought, modern science had not solved the problem of artificial gravity other than some basic improvements, such as the rotating habitation sections on the capital ships.

Colonel West, in his own distinctive armour, moved along the loading section checking on each of the marines.

He certainly looked the part, with his scarred but well cared for armour and a customised L48 rifle on his back.

"We are doing one pass of the docking area. It looks like they have units guarding all the main approaches and have set up anti-aircraft emplacements near the habitation domes. So we're going to have to go in hot and stabilise the situation. First, the gunboats will move in and clear a path through the anti-aircraft mounts, we'll follow and take the docking hub. The rest of the commando units will land at the key points along the hub and loading area. We have four landing craft bringing in our commando company. One landing craft will also bring in an engineering platoon to help with any problems we might face. Once we're inside, our job is to head to the Command Centre so we can shut down the Station's weapon system. Once captured, we need to hold the area and wait for reinforcements. With these down the blockade on Prime will be lifted. Even more importantly, it will allow us to land transports and shuttles to take off survivors. We are expecting anything up to four hundred thousand people here and who knows how many casualties. Until the rest arrive we can expect to be outnumbered by at least ten to one, so we must move fast and hard. Until the weapon systems are offline we can only get a small number of landing craft in. We can't take the entire Station on our own, not even with five hundred could we do it in the time that we have. We have to get the guns offline so General Rivers can bring in the cavalry.

Understood?" he asked.

"Now don't try and bring civilians to the landing craft, we cannot take anybody without a sealed suit and that will probably just be us. Leave the rescue to the jarheads following us in. We do the fighting, the rest of the marines clear up, no exception!" he ordered.

The marines all nodded, some of them hitting their helmets with their ammunition clips. The Colonel then moved further to the front so he could check on their progress. The first wave of the assault consisting of four shuttles and two gunboats went ahead and were just a few kilometres from the Station. Inside their craft a red light started to flash, from their training Spartan knew it meant they were expecting hostile fire.

"Incoming!" shouted one of the commandos at the front over his headset.

A number of fist-sized holes appeared in the outer skin of the landing craft as a long burst of heavy weapons fire raked the craft. Streaks of projectiles blasted past the craft as they moved ever closer. Spartan ducked back, flinching from the incoming fire. The landing craft was heavily armoured as they were designed to get troops to the ground when under fire but these projectiles were substantial. They were obviously expecting trouble.

The nearest gunboat travelled a little further ahead and its weapon pods activated, each one sending clouds of tiny flechette rounds into space that tore the incoming fire to dust. If they had been in atmospheric flight the sounds of weapons fire would have been deafening. But in the silent vacuum of space though there was nothing, just the vibration of the weapons fitted to the ships and the continuous sparks and flashing of them blasting away.

More holes and sparks tore down the left side of the gunboat and then a massive blast tore away one of the thrusters and sent it drifting away from the shuttles.

"Did you see that?" Teresa shouted but her voice was wasted as the intercom system lowered the volume through the built in headsets.

Spartan nodded but he was feeling less confident about this assault by the minute. The small group of craft were less than a kilometre from the Station and as they turned a little to the left Spartan was granted the perfect view of their target. At first it looked like any other moon. It was large and every part of its surface covered in structures, buildings, gantries and shipyards. It served as a colony, naval base, military barracks and transportation hub. Large parts of the colony were burning, presumably from the initial uprising and suicide attacks he had heard about on the news channels. As he watched, he noticed a streak of yellow from several sections of the surface. He squinted, trying to work out what they were before realising they were moving and heading towards them. He turned to warn Teresa but it all happened too fast. As the cloud of incoming fire bounced off the shuttle, the gunboat swung back to rejoin the formation. More fire clattered around both craft and then with a mighty orange flash the gunboat disappeared in a fireball that showered the shuttle with debris and sparks. Spartan was torn from his harness and thrown across the deck against the wall. As soon as his helmet hit the wall he was knocked out cold and slid down to the floor.

Teresa unbuckled herself and crawled along the floor to the unconscious Spartan, the buffeting shuttle shaking her about. More projectiles struck the craft and as she reached out to him three bullets tore through the hull and ripped through her right arm. The velocity of the rounds spun her around and she reached out, grabbing the harness with her left arm.

Marcus spotted the trouble and with great difficulty managed to drag himself over to Teresa. He pulled a sealant pack from the wall and carefully managed to clamp it over the wounded area and the shattered armour. It automatically sealed the gaps and re-pressurised her suit.

"Medic!" he shouted before Teresa really started to feel the pain.

CHAPTER EIGHT

The most famous incident that involved the IMC was the defence of the Confederation Council during the uprising on a desert platform on the planet of Kerberos. The situation was initiated following a trade dispute between a mining company and a transportation guild. During negotiations representatives from the guild brought over four hundred mercenaries from the Rim to capture the Council's delegation.

A single platoon from the warship Spiteful defended the council members until radio contact was lost. When reinforcements arrived, it took them over an hour to work through the bodies of two hundred and twelve mercenaries until they found the bodies of the marines in the main chambers, surrounding the dead council members. It was a terrible loss for the Corps but a day that the Sixth Marine Company has honoured every year since the action. It was from this battle that the elite Guards unit was created with the very role of protecting Confederation officials.

Great Battles of the Confederate Marine Corps

At a distance from the Titan Naval Station, the bloodiest space battle in generations had been continuing for almost half an hour. The massive hulks of the old battleship CCS Victorious and the battlecruiser CCS Crusader had slowed down and were engaged in an epic duel of broadsides. Standing at a distance of several kilometres apart there was almost no chance of their weapons missing and each deadly volley killed scores of crew and smashed great chunks out of the flanks of the vessels. Both ships were trailing debris and fire could be seen at various points in their superstructures but that wasn't anywhere near enough to stop them fighting. The CCS Crusader had placed herself carefully between the enemy vessel and the Titan Naval Station. Her powerful engines and improved mobility over the heavier, slower battleship allowed her to maintain this position, effectively blocking much of the marine assault group that was making its way to the moon.

In the Combat Information Centre, Admiral Jarvis examined the engineering displays as the battle continued around her. Every few moments she lifted her eyes to examine her deadly foe on the projection display on the main wall. By a simple piece of engineering the external camera feeds could recreate the bridge windows from within the armoured safety of the centre deep inside the ship, and it gave the impression she was actually on the bridge of the ship. The damage reports and casualty figures were astounding but so far the newest capital ship in the fleet was doing her job. General Rivers had already left the ship and transferred to the Santa Maria to help conduct the action against Titan Naval Station. Stood next to her was Commander Anderson, her executive officer.

"Admiral, we've taken heavy damage but all our systems are still operational. We are matched in armour and weaponry but we're still not using our trump card, our speed," he said.

"I know, Commander. But we have to keep all of her attention away from the Station though. As soon as General Rivers confirms the commandos' mission, we can reconsider our options here."

"What if we could damage her engines or at the very least reduce her ability to manoeuvre?"

"Like the Bismarck? Yes, I see what you are thinking. She was one of the German Navy's key battleships in the Second World War. Antiquated aircraft damaged her steering, and that made her vulnerable to attack by other warships who then sank her. See what you can do, Commander, in the meantime I want every gun turned to her decks. Smash her!" she ordered.

"Admiral," The officer replied before returning to the

tactical display.

"Lieutenant Nilsson, put me through to General Rivers."

"Yes, Sir."

The connection was almost instant and a pang of pride made her pause for a moment as she considered the speed and quality of her crew. Under no circumstances would she simply throw away this ship and her crew.

"General Rivers, I need an update on your operation, are we on schedule?" she asked.

There was a short delay before the crackling reply came back.

"Admiral, we have started the commando operation. The first landing craft have arrived at the Station and is under very heavy fire," explained the General.

* * *

The loading ring on the Station was littered with debris as the first two platoons of commandos exited their damaged and scarred landing craft. Marcus and another of the commandos helped pulled Spartan and Teresa into cover next to the landing craft before fanning out with the rest of the unit to secure the landing zone. Only two craft had landed so far, the amount of defensive fire having forced the next wave of two craft to redirect to a landing zone almost a kilometre away from where they had landed.

The skill of the pilots was exceptional though and the fact they had managed to land at such high speed, and in once piece, was a testament to their training. The moon had a low level of gravity and a thin atmosphere that required the use of respirators at the very minimum. Not that any of this was a problem for the marines who had training in a variety of gravity scenarios.

The landing area looked much like a waiting lounge in an airport with large open areas and lines of counters for checking in supplies or people. There was also considerable damage within the structure and obvious signs of battle from when the station was seized by the Zealot insurgents. Several heavy haulers, large wheeled vehicles, had crashed into a far wall and some improvised barricades were all that remained of the last ditch attempt to hold onto the place. The marines had fanned out as they pushed their perimeter fifty metres away from the landing craft. Almost as soon as they landed, they had seen fighters rushing out to stop them. The door gunners had held them off spectacularly but a small number of survivors were dug in at the far end of the building and pouring a withering hail of projectiles at the exposed marines. Colonel West and his squad pushed forward and took cover behind a burnt out loading truck, meanwhile the rest of the commandos kept their heads down behind any cover they could find.

Spartan's head was pounding but he could make out the signs of movement. As he tried to focus a series of blasts shook the ground and large debris flew through the bay. It was a bizarre scenario as materials, that on a normal gravity world would barely move, now scattered through the open area as if they were devoid of mass. His focus was almost back to normal and what he could see took him by surprise. Tracer fire whistled past him as the defenders did their best to halt the marines exit from the landing area. Their own return fire was much lighter as they tried to spot their enemies who were well dug in over two hundred metres away. As he pulled himself up he spotted Teresa slumped against the side of the landing craft, protected from the incoming fire.

He moved over, examining her shoulder and spotting the emergency aid pack on her suit. Her eyes looked different, probably due to a mixture of drugs pumping through her body.

"How you doing?" he asked as he checked for any other wounds.

She rolled her head, obviously dazed and unable to do much of use.

"I, uh, my," she said before drifting off again.

Inside his helmet the voices of the squad leaders rocked back and forth as the pinned down marines tried to get out of their difficult position.

"More have arrived, there are about fifteen of them behind the barricades in the access corridor ahead. There's also another group of about fifty coming from the primary habitation ring to the right. Can anybody get to the door guns?" asked the Colonel.

Before anybody could speak the second group unleashed a hail of fire as they ran and bounced along in the low gravity to the marines. As the group rushed ahead the defenders from the barricades stood up and also rushed ahead, joining them in a full assault on the marines' positions.

Spartan, who was just a few metres away from the craft glanced back, checking the vessel. It was heavily damaged and he could see scores of holes along its front and sides. His eyes moved along its length until he came to the weapon mount on the door. There were more holes and a black scorch mark where the gun should be.

"Colonel, Spartan here. The gun on the starboard side is missing. It must have been lost in the landing. I'll check the other side," he said as he climbed inside the craft.

"Don't bother, it is over eighty kilos, you won't be able to do anything useful with it," came back one of the sergeants.

The sound of weapon fire from the marines was now massive as they tried to repel the wave attacks of the suicidal attackers. At least two grenades sailed inside their perimeter, three commandos were badly wounded and knocked out of the fight. More volleys of gunfire blasted across the open area with the odd round striking the thick armour of the landing craft.

Spartan had different ideas though and jumped to the other side of the craft, finding the lower gravity allowed him to take steps he could never normally take. He landed and had to hold on to avoid flying straight out the other side. The weapon mount seemed intact, as did the twin-barrelled machine gun fitted to it. He pulled the locking pins and then with great effort forced the weapon from its mount. Even though the reduced gravity made it feel just over twenty kilos it was still a weighty item. He moved back to the other side of the craft, though now much slower with the added weight and bulk of the weapon system. As he jumped out he met around twenty fanatics with cudgels, knives and other improvised weapons. They had somehow crept around and were trying to outflank them. They were only a few metres away and Spartan, without thinking pulled the trigger on the weapon system. A massive muzzle flash erupted from the gun as it poured hundreds of large calibre explosive rounds at the unarmoured attackers. The impact was instant and brutal as limbs, heads and torsos were smashed apart by the finger-sized projectiles. Even more sickening was that as each round impacted on their flesh it triggered a tiny explosive that had enough power to vaporise the flesh within ten centimetres in each direction. The flanking attack was over as soon as it had began and Spartan found himself pinned against the side of the landing craft, the massive recoil on the weapon forcing him back.

He looked out at the trail of gore he had created and then down to Teresa who was looking up, her eyes a little clearer and a wicked grin on her face.

"You crazy son of a bitch!" she laughed.

There was no time for conversation as the Colonel was quickly voicing his concerns on the intercom.

"They're going to overrun us, use everything you've got, we have to drive them back!" he barked.

Spartan pulled himself from the wall and after checking Teresa was in a secure spot, moved around the landing craft and to where the thin line of commandos was pinned down. He moved ahead and dumped the weapon mount on top of a shattered hydraulic loader. Colonel West turned to him and then pointed at the enemy.

"Marine, is that thing working?" he asked loudly.

Spartan nodded and with great effort leaned against the gun, doing his best to brace against the expected recoil and then pulled the trigger. As before, the muzzle blast was vast. The guns were not designed for use by infantry, their expected role was fire support during landing or evacuation. Though the recoil was great, this time Spartan controlled the bursts, easing off before it became too great and knocked him over. His first two bursts were a little high but the subsequent ones were deadly. The three closest insurgents who were heading to the landing craft, were shredded into pulp and the ones behind them scattered trying to find cover from the heavy machine gun. It was all pointless though, as Spartan hunted down each and every one of them. The large calibre explosive rounds made easy work until all that remained was one fighter who was pinned behind one of the wrecked loading trucks. The Colonel raised his hand, indicating an immediate ceasefire. As the weapons stopped and the dust and debris cleared, the carnage of the battle became clear. Blood and bone littered the ground as burn marks and small fires ran throughout the structure. One of the new recruits stood up, for a moment forgetting about the lone fighter. Before he could move, a single round pierced the front of his helmet and slammed him backwards, instantly killing him.

Colonel West lifted his L48 rifle and locked in the range to the sniper's cover. With a quick flick of the weapon he fired off three large calibre explosive rounds. He ducked back down as the projectiles hit. Just as in the training exercises the weapon did its job beautifully but this was the first time Spartan had seen the effects of the live rounds. The man had hidden safely behind the thick metal, but the Colonel had fired slightly above him. As the projectile appeared over his head, there was a flash and the upper half of the man vaporised in a spray of blood and organs. Colonel West did a quick scan of the area and then stood up.

"Marines, move it, we are nine hundred metres from the Command Centre. Go, go, go!" he screamed at them.

The officer and his squad rushed ahead and were quickly followed by the rest of the marines except for two who stayed behind to tend the wounded. Spartan dumped the now empty weapon mount on the ground and jumped back to Teresa. She was already getting up, the drugs must have been working, as she almost seemed back to herself. One of the marine medics moved over, checking her injuries with a scanner.

"You should stay with the landing craft, the damage is serious but not fatal," he explained.

"Good," she replied as she pulled her rifle from her shoulder down into a low position.

"Ready?" she asked.

Spartan knew better than to argue and quickly moved ahead to follow the rest of the marines who were pushing on. With the lower gravity Teresa was able to keep up without straining her injured shoulder as much as she would have expected, it seemed the painkillers were masking much of the pain.

The survivors of the two squads pushed on and apart from sporadic fire from the odd hidden insurgent, they made quick progress from the loading bay and deep into the main corridor leading to the central plaza. From there, there were multiple paths leading to the commerce exchange and main Council Chamber that operated as a kind of central governmental building for the Station. Colonel West examined a detailed structural model on the display in his helmet, checking for the access points and possible weaknesses. The Military Command Centre was built onto the back of the Council Chambers. They would either have to fight through the building, or work their way around the back and through the Naval Academy to reach the Command Centre. His decision was cut short as they rounded the final corner. A flurry of gunshots blasted towards them from a hastily erected barricade that was flung across the entire front side of the square. One marine was cut down and Colonel West only avoided fire by jumping high and throwing himself over a wall as he hit it a metre off the ground.

The area in front of the Council Chambers was a vast square, packed with now ruined monuments and waterfalls. It was the most photogenic part of the Station and often used when visiting dignitaries arrived. Along the one side at least a dozen vehicles were abandoned and being used as part of the barricades. From the upper floors of the concrete neoclassical building a number of shooters fired rifles and carbines from windows and openings.

Colonel West kept going, knowing that if they held back they would be picked off, one by one. As he moved, the remnants of the two squads moved with him, each marine spreading out and firing from the shoulder as they bounced and ran. It was a peculiar sight to see, as they skipped, ran and jumped, because of the reduced gravity in the Station. Multiple explosions indicated rockets being fire at them as they pushed ahead. Three marines were killed by the time they reached the barricades, but then the situation changed completely.

The Colonel was first over the next wall and crashed down between two Zealots. He slammed his rifle butt into the first, the impact smashing his face and forcing him back several metres. As more marines leapt over the barricades, he moved to his left and fired three rounds into the next fighter's chest. The rounds shattered his torso and sent chunks of flesh across the ground as the man was brutally slaughtered. The Colonel turned, making sure the rest of his men were in position. As he looked around he noted with satisfaction that the marines were doing well. Bayonets, knives and rifles were all used as the two squads hacked and blasted their way through the line. Spartan, Teresa and three more marines appeared at the far left of the barricade and with just a handful of shots eliminated the Zealots trying to retreat inside the Council Chambers.

"Don't stop, keep up the pressure!" The Colonel shouted as he rushed ahead.

As the officer entered the large arched entrance there was a bright flash and the entire front section of the building collapsed in a series of explosions and flashes of fire. The force of the blast knocked most of the marines to the ground and Spartan was shielded from the explosion by one of the pillars directly in front of him. As he edged closer, he could see over a hundred fighters pouring out of the council building through the breaches in the now shattered structure. He stood firmly, lifted his rifle to his shoulder and started to fire, each round shredding the Zealots as they rushed out to attack. Teresa moved up and joined in, adding her fire to the surge of fighters. The rest of the marines dragged themselves up but several were cut down before they could even stand. Rather than engage in a firefight the crowd of fanatics overwhelmed the marines and within seconds the entire section in front of the Council Chamber devolved into a murderous melee. In the ruins, the mortally wounded Colonel dragged himself clear of the rubble and looked down at where his legs should be. The improvised explosives had torn them away as well as leaving a gaping wound in his flank. He tried to draw his pistol from his thigh holster but his arm refused to obey. He turned his head and watched in a mixture of awe and dread as Spartan and the surviving marines fought their desperate and bloody battle. His last image was of Spartan swinging a bladed weapon of some kind and cutting down two Zealots in one blow.

"You crazy son of a bitch!" he muttered before passing out.

* * *

The battle between the two great naval juggernauts continued and it appeared that the older battleship was taking slightly more damage. The battle was hardly one of skills and tactics. It was simply a battle of engineers, gunners and firepower as each ship tried to put out more firepower than the other over a given time. The old battleship was starting to inch its way back to the Naval Station but with the damage both ships were taking neither could move quickly.

"Admiral, she's moving, we can't shield the Station from this range," said Commander Anderson.

Admiral Jarvis examined the tactical screen in detail as well as the engineering section. She had her hand raised to her face and it looked as if she was trying to mentally crunch a large volume of numbers.

"How many marines do we have on board?" she asked.

The Commander was taken aback for a moment, as his brain seemed to block the answer to such a simple question. He shook his head as the numbers returned.

"Uh, three companies of marines, most of them are assisting in the medical bays," he replied.

"What do you think of our reports on the experimental Sanlav Rounds?" she asked with a raised eyebrow.

"Sanlav Rounds? The experimental canister shots, Admiral?"

The Admiral nodded as she waited for his thoughts.

"Well, from the reports they seem excellent at damaging or destroying light to medium armour at range. What they lack in depth penetration they gain in a wider damage pattern. What are you thinking, Admiral?" he asked unsure what to expect.

"We need to keep her from the Station but we won't do it with guns alone. My suggestion is a simple one but it has been done well enough in the past. We double-charge batteries, use our speed to close the distance and give her a broadside at point-blank range. With that amount of fire we should be able to reduce her crew numbers, if not her weapon system, and clear the way for a boarding party," she said.

"Boarding party? You mean to take her?" he said incredulously.

"No, no, we don't have the time or the manpower for that. All we need to do is disable her engines."

"Or her power plant, Admiral. Without power she will be dead in the water and weaponless," he added.

"Excellent, so we rake her flank, board her and then cripple her power plant. Outstanding!" she said with a grin.

The Admiral turned from her executive officer and towards Lieutenant Nilsson.

"Lieutenant, get me Lieutenant Erdeniz, I believe he is on the gun deck," she ordered.

* * *

Deep in the fighting decks of the Crusader the gun crews

maintained the weapon systems and kept the ship in the battle. Lieutenant Erdeniz, although still wearing his bandages from injuries sustained in the attempted revolt on the ship, was standing at his post. Though there were metres of armour and two more decks between him and the CCS Victorious it was still a terrifying experience. In the last twenty minutes there had been two major breaches and the second one had vaporised one of his gunners before his eyes. This part of the ship was superheated and everybody working there was dripping in sweat.

His information on the rest of the ship was limited but he had seen the medical figures and it was clear to all onboard that the medical bays were to be avoided unless absolutely critical. His best guess was that they had already sustained two or three hundred dead with about the same number injured. It was high losses and as each member of the crew was removed from action the workload for those left increased. His crew of twenty-four engineers, gunners and loaders had already been whittled down to nineteen with one battery knocked out of action, three dead and two badly wounded.

"How are we doing?" he asked as he moved along the gantry checking on the three remaining gun batteries.

"Third battery is running hot, we've got maybe four or five volleys left and I'll need to swap the rails out," replied Gunner Thomas.

"Are you sure, can you reduce the power and keep them

running?" asked the Lieutenant.

"Well, we could but that will cut the velocity down to half, Sir," he replied as he turned, waiting for an answer.

"Do it, we can't afford to take any chances in this fight. Maintenance can wait, right now every gun needs to keep firing!" he gave the order.

The wall-mounted intercom alarm started to blare, indicating that the command staff needed to speak with him. He moved off the gantry and down to the main command terminal.

"Lieutenant Erdeniz here," he said loudly.

* * *

Spartan was covered in blood, his armoured suit was a bizarre mixture of camouflage pattern, dirt and the red streaks of gore. His L48 rifle was on the floor, its clip expended and the bayonet had snapped and was embedded in one of the insurgents' chests. He had his left arm locked around the throat of one man as his right wielded a vicious looking machete that he had torn from one of the many fanatics that had attacked them. One of the few surviving men suddenly rushed towards him and with a fast, almost callous, slash he removed the attacker's head clean from his torso. Following up with a slick twist on his left arm he broke man's neck, dropping him to the ground like a piece of discarded garbage. Teresa was down on one knee as she smashed her rifle butt into the side of a wounded fighter's head before lifting the weapon up and putting two rounds into another. Off to the left Jesus, Marcus and three other marines were fighting the last four fanatics, easily cutting them down with their weapons.

There were now only twelve commandos still able to fight and as they staggered forward, they dragged the rest of the wounded marines into cover. The bodies of many of them were buried deep under the scores of dead fanatics. As they were tending the casualties Marcus found the badly wounded Colonel West. The man's body was shattered, his legs torn away and a huge trail of blood all around him. Marcus dropped to one knee, checking the officer's suit for any signs of life. Incredibly he picked up a faint pulse.

Sergeant Williams limped over and knelt down next to the wounded man.

"Sir, Colonel, can you hear me?" he called.

The Sergeant reached out gently shaking him. The Colonel moved but he was unable to speak. Spartan looked back at the wounded and then ahead to their objective, noting they were now only a short distance away. He was torn between helping this officer and getting the mission done.

"Sergeant, we have to shut off those guns. The only way the Colonel is getting out alive is if we can get the rest of the regiment here."

As if to remind them of the urgency of their situation a small group of insurgents appeared from the far right of the plaza and moved towards the their position. They were a mixture of well-equipped Zealot fighters and lightly armed fanatics, probably reinforcements from the surface. The group fired a few shots as they rushed ahead, the projectiles ricocheting from the walls around them. But without stopping and correcting their aim the fire was sporadic and inaccurate. A heavy weapon tore chunks from the wall behind them and one of the rounds hit Marcus below the knee, it sent him crashing to the ground crying out in pain.

The Sergeant put his hand on Spartan's shoulder.

"Do it, we'll watch your back!" he said, before turning around and helping the wounded Marcus into a ragged firing line behind the rubble and bodies. He quickly placed an emergency first aid pack on his shattered leg and then started firing at the approaching enemy. Two of the less seriously injured men helped to move the badly wounded Colonel to cover before joining the firing line.

"Everybody else come with me, we have work to do!" Spartan shouted.

The filthy and blood spattered marines moved on, with Spartan, Teresa and Jesus taking the lead through the now ruined building. Though most of them were still carrying their L48 rifles, Spartan and two others were holding a mixture of close quarter weapons. In this cramped and filthy environment they appeared to be just as useful. Once they were through the entrance they rushed along the main foyer and then down the side corridor. According to Spartan's tactical display this would take them to the rear yard and on to the Command Centre. There was a chance that this part of the building would be booby-trapped, they could only hope that the first blast and collapse had already triggered any further devices. Either way it didn't matter, time wasn't on their side. If they waited any longer they would be overrun as more of the insurgents made their way to the area and surrounded the small number of marines. They needed to get the weapons off-line and help get the reinforcements into battle as quickly as possible.

Two Zealots lay in wait and as they reached the back entrance, they opened fire. As the bullets flew around them Spartan rolled to one side just as Jesus and Teresa hit the attackers with well-aimed shots. They didn't stop and in seconds they were in the open and running in a loose line to the gatehouse at the front of the Command Centre. It was normally protected by a strong perimeter wall and gate, but now there were multiple breaches and none of the usual security. Spartan slid into cover behind the ruins of the wall and focused his helmet-mounted optics on the Command Centre. Zooming in he examined the defences and sighed in anger as he hit the communication trigger on his helmet.

"This is Private Spartan, our commando unit has made

it to the Command Centre. Colonel West is down, there are twelve of us left," he said on the radio.

The radio crackled with a broken signal from the Santa Maria.

"Spartan, good work. Third platoon is pinned down, the engineers have made it to the side-loading bay at the Command Centre, one hundred metres from the secondary entrance. If you can get to them they should be able to find you a way in."

Spartan turned to his right, squinting through the dust and debris. He couldn't see any movement, then he spotted the five armoured engineers stomping towards the Command Centre. All five were covered in dents and scorch marks and they had obviously had a very difficult time making it this far.

"I see them, we're on the way!" Spartan said, as he indicated to the rest of his squad.

They were instantly moving around the compound and towards the engineers. The defenders had already noticed the noisy, armoured marines and were pouring fire into them. One rocket blasted past and impacted near the leading marine and sent him crashing to the ground. He was up fast though and kept moving ahead. They were only twenty metres away now and Spartan contacted the closest on the intercom.

"4th Squad, can you bring down the wall?" he asked.

The lead marine in the heavy armour turned briefly to

see Spartan and his squad emerge from the debris and fan out around the engineers.

"Nice to see you!" he said with a genuine sound of happiness in his voice. "If you can keep their heads down we'll do the rest," he said.

The arrival of the extra manpower gave them the cover they needed and with one final push the engineer unit surged ahead, leaping over the ruined perimeter wall and up to the thick masonry of the Command Centre. The defenders tried to hold them back but concentrated fire from Spartan's squad kept their heads down.

The first marine slammed his armoured fist into the stone around the secondary doorway and ripped a metre long section from it. The second moved in and after several strikes tore a hole large enough to crawl inside. The two then grabbed the sides of the breach and tore them back, making a large hole in the wall to expose the dozen or so defenders to the wrath of the marines. As soon as the hole appeared, Jesus and Teresa tossed grenades inside. They rushed ahead, taking cover each side of hole. From inside they could hear panic as the unarmoured defenders tried desperately to avoid the weapons.

With a crump the hole filled with dust and bright flames rushed out. Spartan entered first and found only three dazed men still standing. He slashed the first across the throat as he struck the second with his fist. The heavy impact sent the man stumbling backwards and into a chair before he collapsed to the ground. Spartan pushed on inside as Teresa leapt in and dealt with the final man. Seeing the woman approach the fanatic gave her a wicked snigger and took a step forward to strike. Teresa simply blasted his leg, sending him crashing to the floor. Before he could try to respond she dropped down and embedded her bayoneted L48 rifle into his heart.

The two moved inside and the rest of the commandos followed. Several of them dealt with the wounded in their own particular style before the area was fully cleared. As Spartan stood in the room, he could see a long hallway decked with computer systems. However, none appeared to be connected to the high security weapons system. From his blueprints it said the weapon system was placed right here in its protected environment. He moved along, checking each as he went while the rest of the commandos spread out to secure the centre. Reaching the end he found a large iron-coloured blast door with a red light flashing next to it. A glowing sign above it simply read 'Weapons Control'.

"Shit!" swore Spartan, as he realised there was no way he could get through such a massive structure, certainly not in hurry.

"Come on, we need a way in, this is what we're here for!" he shouted.

Teresa took a step forward before looking up to Spartan. "How about the engineers?"

She moved closer as she looked around the perimeter of the door, trying to find a weakness. The door was extremely well made and there were no discernable gaps between the wall and the metal of the door itself.

A hissing sound came from the door and to their astonishment it lifted up to reveal the control room with all of its systems undamaged and fully operation. They both turned back to see Jesus sat at one of the desks and working on the computer terminal.

"Jesus?" asked Spartan.

"Hey, man, like I told you, I've got skills!" he said laughing.

Spartan smiled and then stepped inside the room, their primary objective. He sat down in front of the main computer system and scanned the options available to him. From there he could access the landing grid, point defence weapons and orbital guns. He tapped on the orbital guns and a menu appeared offering him a variety of options from powering up, testing and firing sequences. He selected the off-line mode and a message popped up along with a series of images showing each of the guns disarming and reverting to safe mode. Satisfied that it was working he called back the Santa Maria.

"Spartan here, we've accessed the Weapons Control Centre, the system should be fully off-line in less than one minute," he said with satisfaction.

"Excellent work. Private, the cavalry are on the way.

Get your people back to the loading bays, we will have shuttles there for you shortly."

Teresa turned to Spartan and gave him a thumbs up, things were starting to go their way.

CHAPTER NINE

Since the founding of the new colonies the status of Old Earth and its solar system became less important. The colonies at Alpha Centauri quickly matched and then surpassed the old world. As further colonies spread through the Centauri Constellation the balance of power shifted leaving Earth as a distant backwater. Though it was still the centre of old culture and knowledge it transformed over generations into just one of many backwater systems inhabited by those unable or unwilling to leave. Following the Great War, the Centauri Confederation was founded with each colony world being made an equal of the next. In one swift move, Old Earth became just another colony in an alliance that no longer even shared its name.

The Decline of Earth

The guns were silent and like a swarm of locusts the assault transports and shuttles from the Santa Maria and the Santa Cruz filled the gulf between the ships and the Titan Naval Station. A total of sixteen hundred heavily equipped marines were spread in over thirty craft. The transports were the largest, each one carrying a full company of marines and their heavy weapons. The shuttles brought in small, more specialist squads as well as equipment and medical supplies. Another hundred marines were waiting onboard the Santa Cruz as a quick response team in case of emergencies. As they approached the Station they split into small groups, each one targeting key parts of the complex where survivors were likely to be. As the craft reached a kilometre from the Station a small amount of defensive fire erupted, primarily from small arms and a handful of larger calibre weapons. No craft were lost and within seconds the first wave crashed down on the surface and released the eager troops.

At the Command Centre, Spartan and the surviving commandos had done sterling work though they had no time to enjoy it. So far, they had brought the guns down and the Station's computer systems were being used to pinpoint the surviving population. They had already transmitted the life sign scans of the habitation and naval facilities, but there was no way to determine whether they were friendly or hostile. That was something the advancing marines would have to discover for themselves.

There was still sporadic gunfire outside the Command Centre but with the late arrival of the third commando squad they had been able to establish a strong perimeter to protect the site. The engineers were also still moving chunks of masonry to reinforce their position until they were able to leave. With the arrival of the missing squad was also Lieutenant Daniels, a young but aggressive officer whom Spartan had never seen before. He had immediately taken charge of the situation and had shown a degree of deference to Spartan and the work of his group.

"Captain Mathews here, we have evacuated Colonel West and most of your wounded by shuttlecraft," came a transmission to the Lieutenant.

"Thank you, Sir, we are well entrenched but are still under sporadic attack," he explained.

"I have four companies of marines making their way to you. You can't leave yet though, I have orders from General Rivers. From the data sent over by Private Spartan it would appear the closest habitation section to you is housing approximately two hundred people. Can you put him on, Lieutenant?" he asked.

"Sir, I have the data right here," replied the officer as he lowered his voice, obviously trying to keep the conversation to himself.

"No, I need it from the source and as I understand it, Spartan and his unit have been working through the data for the last twenty minutes!" he said and his tone was becoming strained.

"Uh, yes, Sir, one moment," said the officer as he was walking back along the corridor and into the large computer suite.

"Spartan, Captain Mathews for you," he said.

Spartan was slumped in a large chair as he worked through the screen of data. Jesus was in his element and had already patched in the security feeds and climate control monitors to help gauge the level of people and resistance at key points in the Station. He was currently tracing a series of energy spikes in the Station power plant and so far none of them could work out why they were happening or where large segments of the power was being sent. Spartan hit the button on his built-in intercom, instantly patching him into the radio conversation.

"Spartan here, how can I help you, Sir?"

"Spartan, we've secured the first survivors and are moving into the zones you've provided the data for. I've received word from the General that suggests the energy surges you've identified are coming from the fusion plants in the naval yard," he explained.

Spartan turned to Jesus.

"Jesus, can you bring up the power schematics of the naval yard and forward them to the General?" he asked.

"Doing it!" Jesus replied as he skimmed through the screen on his terminal.

As Spartan turned around, he wondered to himself

where the man's computing skills had come from and why he was in the Marine Corps. Of course, it was pretty simple though, a man who could work these systems could earn a fortune both legitimately or otherwise. He had no doubts on the direction Jesus would have taken. He allowed himself a small grin as he called back to the Captain.

"Captain, we're sending the data to the General, I think you might be right, though. It seems there is a lot of energy building up. You think they have something down there?" he asked.

"One moment, Spartan, we'll be with you shortly, please let the Lieutenant have your men hold your fire, we're approaching your compound," said the Captain.

Spartan lifted himself up from the chair and bounded towards the damaged doorway.

"Lieutenant, the marines are here, Captain Mathews has asked you ensure our men watch their fire."

The two men went outside and to the improvised firing line where the commandos had established a strong outer perimeter. Spartan dropped down behind the rubble and scanned the distant debris. He could see the odd movement as the insurgents redeployed in their attempts to work their way around them. As he watched a smoke trail rush towards them and crashed into the side of the Command Centre. The blast tore a hole several metres wide and brought a pile of dust and debris down into the outer compound.

Spartan picked up his reloaded L48 rifle and fired a series of short bursts, each cluster of rounds striking at any point where the muzzle flashes appeared. A group of four Zealots broke cover, attempting to close the distance, but the impact from the large calibre shells slammed the first to the floor. As he dropped the first man to the ground two more bullets exploded at the preset distance sending shards of metal into the torsos of the other three.

More groups appeared from their hiding places as if a number of beaters were moving prey to the waiting hunters. Then a series of yellow flashes and a great cloud of dust signalled the arrival of the rest of the marines. As they came from out of the rubble Spartan could see scores of the men bounding forward towards the Command Centre. In the centre of the group a man carried a small flexible regimental standard. It was a bizarre look of modern personal protection suits and archaic symbols of a medieval battlefield. The horde of marines easily cut their way through the disorganised Zealots and moved up and around the Command Centre. A small group led by the Captain approached Lieutenant Daniels who immediately stood to attention and saluted. He looked to his side, looking at the perimeter and the dirt and blood-splattered commandos.

"Sterling work, people, outstanding!" he said beaming.

Teresa appeared at the entrance of the building,

shouting over to Spartan.

"We've got a problem!" she shouted and then ducked back inside.

Spartan turned from the firing line and rushed in through the doorway, closely followed by the two officers. As they moved towards the computer room, the first thing that was evident was that half the displays and computer systems were offline. As they watched a number of the screens shutdown.

"We're losing them, one by one," Jesus said as he frantically tried to isolate several of the systems before the lot went down.

Crackling in their headsets signalled a message from General Rivers.

"All company commanders, this is an urgent message. We are detecting explosions in the main reactor cores. According to our calculations, the insurgents are triggering a station-wide series of explosions that will destroy it. You have no more than forty minutes to get your people and as many survivors off as possible. I repeat, you have forty minutes to evacuate. We're sending every shuttle we can find to you. Get out of there!" he barked.

Captain Mathews rubbed his jaw as he considered the situation.

"General, what is the status on the civilian population?" he asked.

"So far we have taken off sixty-two percent of those

we are aware of. There are still three habitation zones, including yours, left to clear. We have spotted insurgents all around your position, expect heavy resistance if you try to reach them, just don't be late!" said the General.

"Can we do it?" asked the Captain.

"We can't clear the habitation area and get back to the landing craft in forty minutes, we have to choose one or the other," answered Spartan.

"How about we wait at the habitation zone for reinforcements to pick us up?" Lieutenant Daniels asked.

"You're assuming there is anybody that can reach us in time," replied the Captain before calling to the Santa Maria.

"General, how long till those reinforcements get here?"

"We have a final shuttle group on its way, it will be landing in approximately thirty minutes."

"Can you redirect everybody to the Central Habitation Zone Plaza? There is enough space to land shuttles and we can evacuate the entire section from there," asked the Captain.

"Interesting, yes, it should be possible. I'll see if I can get a few transports to redirect to you, good luck, Captain."

"There won't be enough transports to take off all the marines and the civilians," said Lieutenant Daniels.

"There is another option," said Spartan.

"All squad commanders prepare to move out," said the Captain before turning to Spartan. "I'm listening," he said.

"Give the Lieutenant one of your companies to clear the route back and get the landing craft. If they can do it in less than thirty minutes, they can get the rest of the landing craft and meet us at the central plaza. That should give us enough capacity to load the civilians and get out of here."

"Can you get back with one company?" asked the Captain.

"Yes, Sir, no problem," replied Lieutenant Daniels.

The Captain thought about the plan but only for a few seconds, decisive action was needed.

"Okay, Lieutenant, make your way back and get the boats to the plaza."

Daniels turned and ran outside, though he was a lower rank than would be expected, he was a commando junior officer and the marines instantly recognised him as such. It was just seconds before the company were moving away and back towards the landing craft.

"Ok, Spartan, the rest of us will split into three groups, I'll take the two main groups directly to the habitation zone, it's two, three minutes tops from here. I want you to take two squads plus the rest of your commandos and take the right sector. You'll be entering through the ruined bar and then hit them from the side. Get in there hard and fast, we don't have much time," he said.

"They aren't my men," Spartan said as he prepared his gear.

"They are now, Spartan, I'm giving you a temporary field promotion to Sergeant, now get going!" he said with a grin.

"Sir!" shouted Spartan before turning to see a grinning Jesus staring at him.

* * *

The CCS Crusader approached almost point blank range of the damaged battleship Victorious. Both vessels were still moving ever closer to the Titan Naval Station and it was critical that the battleship was stopped, one way or the other. A boarding action between two such vessels had never been attempted but that wasn't going to stop Admiral Jarvis. As the battlecruiser moved into position her guns were silent. Unknown to the crew of the Victorious she was charging up her weapons for one final, overpowered volley of fire. This meant she was exposed to four more volleys of fire before she was in position.

As the two massive ships approached to within two hundred metres, a final broadside from each ship crashed into both vessels. At this range the damage was horrendous and hole after hole appeared along the length of the battlecruiser. It still wasn't enough though and the leviathan slid into position, her gun ports waiting to unleash their deadly new weapon. This time the Crusader made use of her double-charged railgun to fire the modified and lethal close range Sanlav round. It was the first test of the weapon and at this range the damage was nothing short of impressive. Like a giant shotgun the railguns blast a wide dispersal, that at such a short range tore chunks from the outer plating along the entire length of the battleship. With a massive cloud of debris blocking the view, the magnetic couplers powered up, drawing the vessels towards each other. In less than twenty seconds the two ships crunched together and like a privateer in the seventeenth century the Crusader jammed herself tightly against the enemy vessel. The only way the two ships would now be sprung apart was if both took their couplers offline and this was something that could be decided by the first ever capital ship boarding action.

In the Combat Information Centre Admiral Jarvis watched her screens as the Sanlav rounds did their work. Several of the weapon batteries were taken off-line by the brutal overloaded attack, but it had done its work. As well as tearing the great chunks out of the outer skin of the Victorious, the weapon had created a screen of dust, debris and plasma that gave her the cover she needed for her boarding action.

"All marine units, boarding action is a go, commence your assault. Good luck!" she exclaimed over the intercom.

From key points along the hull of the Crusader a dozen landing craft rushed out to transport their precious cargos of marines to the battleship. There were only three hundred marines and another two hundred volunteers from the crew in the attack but they were all targeting one point on the ship, the power core, the only target they could assault with any hope of slowing the warship.

* * *

Lieutenant Erdeniz kept his head down as the landing craft he was in dashed across the short distance between the two capital ships. He and the rest of the passengers all wore sealed suits, but the gear he wore was the bulky variant designed for extra vehicular activity when working on the ship. It was not the closer fitting personal protection suits of the marines. Most of the decks' gunnery crews had been selected to provide assistance to the marines during the boarding action. It was the duty of all crew to practice basic hand-to-hand combat and marksmanship for such eventualities but he had never expected he would have to help in such a situation. Unlike the marines he was armed with a thermal shotgun, a powerful close ranged firearm but it was nothing as effective as the L48 rifles and carbines carried by the rest of the marines.

With a jarring impact the landing craft smashed through the damaged outer skin of the battleship and continued on until embedding itself fifteen metres inside the wrecked metal. Their objective was specifically chosen so they could insert the marines directly into the crew area of the ship. The front of the landing craft pushed though the sidewall of one of the service corridors. The onboard sensors indicated a partial pressurised area, but it was still failing and like most of the ship, lacked gravity.

The bow doors opened to reveal the damage and the marines were already out, each using their hands or their manoeuvring thrusters to push on inside. According to the schematics of the battleship they should be near the main engineering hub that connected to key parts of the ship.

It was hard work to fight through the debris as well as trying to manage the lack of gravity and the bulky suit. As he moved, he positioned himself over the corridor and then activated his grav boots. With a clunk, he found himself walking on the surface though it soon became clear he was upside down as he pushed forwards. About ten metres ahead the marines gathered around a sealed door. From the plans, it was one of the many sealed sections of the ship. One man was already running a bypass on it whilst the rest had their weapons at the ready. With a jarring sound, the door slid across to reveal the main access corridor that led to the engineering hub. As they made to move inside a series of bright streaks rushed past him. Lieutenant Erdeniz jumped to the sidewall as the projectiles blasted past. One of the marines took multiple rounds in the chest. The impact of the weapon's fire propelled him backwards.

"Go, marines!" The sergeant shouted over his intercom.

The first group pushed ahead, each man firing his weapon as he went. It was a surreal sight as the violence of the battle compared with the silence of space. The lack of sound didn't cut the noise of the shouting and orders that constantly blared through his intercom.

* * *

Spartan and his small group of marines and commandos had made good progress in working their way across the Station. So far, they had run into just three insurgents and each had been dealt with quickly and quietly. After the bloody work of landing at the Station, the commandos seemed almost relaxed as they worked their way through the ruins of the old bar. Being so close to the habitation zone, they had to be as quiet as they were able and that meant using close quarter weapons or silencers when possible. As they moved past the ruined wooden bar several men and a bloodied woman leapt from cover. They managed to drag one of the marines down to the ground and proceeded to stab at him repeatedly with a stiletto-like knife. Spartan waded in, slamming his heavy boot into the woman's chest and sending her flying back against the side of the bar. One of the commandos grabbed the arm of the closest man and jammed his fighting knife into his collar. He then pulled the blade out and struck several more times before letting the body slide to the floor. The rest of the squad made quick work of the rest before pushing on to the far side of the bar. As they reached the back section they moved more slowly, each well aware that on the other side could be scores, even hundreds of people. They inched along until Teresa found a crack in the wall that gave him a large enough gap to look though. As he peered inside his helmet-mounted headset crackled.

"I'm at the landing zone, there is a group of about forty insurgents on your way, we picked off the last few but the rest made it past us, watch your backs. We should be airborne in five minutes, will meet you at the rendezvous," said Lieutenant Daniels on the intercom.

Spartan looked back, he couldn't see any trouble but he wasn't taking any chances. He sent four of the marines back to the rubble to keep an eye on their rear.

Looking back inside through a small gap in the wall he could see hundreds of people huddled in groups throughout the courtyard section of the habitation zone. The area was like a large dormitory with lots of rooms surrounding an open courtyard. Three or four Zealots guarded each group and there were large numbers of more guarding the doorways that led into the zone. Also there were more of them higher up, probably armed with sniper rifles to cover the courtyard.

"Captain, we're in position, have you received our tactical data?" he asked.

"Good work, Sergeant, we will assault the four main entrances. We'll start with a flashbang storm and then rush it. As soon as the firefight begins, I need you to clear the snipers and then move to the guards around the prisoners. Assault starts in twenty seconds."

"Understood, Sir," replied Spartan.

* * *

The boarding party had pushed past the lightly defended engineering hub and had progressed to just thirty metres from the power plant core when they came across heavy resistance. Dug in all around the engineering section almost thirty Zealots had rushed to defend the critical core of the ship. Unlike their normal aggressive tactics, they held back with each one taking cover and doing their best to hold off the marines. They ducked behind the thickly armoured coolant tanks and pipes that ran all through this sector of the ship. The battle looked bizarre as most of them were using their grav boots to stand on the walls, floor and ceiling. It made the battle both fluid and highly confusing to Lieutenant Erdeniz. Volley after volley poured down the corridor and every time one of the marines tried to push ahead, they were blasted back by the weapons' fire.

"Shit!" barked the sergeant on the intercom. "We need heavy weapons here, we're pinned down," he shouted, though none of the marines seemed to know what to do. They were going nowhere.

Lieutenant Erdeniz leaned around the corner and fired several shots from his thermal shotgun. It looked impressive but he had no idea if he hit anything. He looked at the clip, noting he had only half the clip remaining. It was useless, at this rate they would end up surrounded. He looked around in the vain hope of finding something more dangerous than his shotgun. It was then that he saw the technician's terminal behind the blast hatch on the left side of the corridor.

"Sergeant, I might be able to short out the coolants units, it could give us the break we need," he called over the radio.

One of the marines tried to help the Lieutenant to the other side but another volley of shot blasted down hitting him in the arm and throwing him back in pain. The Sergeant could see what was happening and without hesitating, gave the order.

"Give him covering fire, now!" he ordered.

Seven marines pushed out from behind cover, each of them firing shot after shot at the enemy. Their fire was inaccurate and the Lieutenant saw only one of the enemy take a hit to the torso, before he was manhandled across the corridor and in front of the terminal. More fire blasted behind him that caught the Sergeant and another marine directly in the face.

Lieutenant Erdeniz did his best to ignore the ongoing carnage and pulled open the hatch. He needed the use of his hands and had to release several of the EVA seals on his suit to release his arms. They were still sealed inside his skin-tight protective suit but nothing like the armour the marines wore. One good stab with a knife could penetrate the skin of this clothing. He looked at the display carefully. Though he couldn't shut down the power plant he could alter the controls that regulated part of the power grid and cooling. Luckily, his computing skills were significant enough for him to isolate and boost the coolant controls to overload. Warnings came up immediately but he easily overrode them and embedded a lockout on the engineering panel. Only a senior officer could override his work and even then the officer would have to make it down to engineering. It wasn't perfect but he had bought them some time.

Turning to the rest of the marines and crew from the battlecruiser he gave a hand signal so the men ducked down and kept out of the line of fire. Corporal Jones moved up from further along the corridor, he held his L48 carbine at the ready.

"How long, Lieutenant?" asked the Corporal.

"Fifteen seconds!" Lieutenant Erdeniz shouted back.

"Take cover, when the tanks blow everybody move forward, no matter the cost. We have to secure the power plant!" ordered the Corporal.

They all pulled themselves into any cover they could find as the odd single shot tore down the corridor. There were now dozens of marines and crew all huddling down as they waited for the coolant tanks. Fifteen seconds passed and nothing happened. The Corporal turned to the officer, he was about to start shouting when a great burst of gas rushed down the corridor.

"Go!" he shouted, and in moments the corridor was packed with scores of people trying to fight their way into the area. Fire scattered around them but the mixture of gas, steam and debris gave them enough cover to get a handful of marines into position.

Lieutenant Erdeniz moved ahead as bodies tumbled about him from both sides. He grabbed onto the wall pulling himself clear of the carnage and kept tugging until he reached the far side of the room where the defenders had been holding out. Further ahead was a dark room with a dull red glow flashing in sequence. He recognised it immediately. The Corporal had somehow survived the devastation and pulled himself up to Lieutenant Erdeniz.

"Is that it?" he asked.

Lieutenant Erdeniz nodded at the Corporal who sighed with relief.

"Get the thermite charges here now, everybody else clear the route to the boats, once they're set we are out of here!"

The two dropped to the deck and, using their grav

boots, made quick progress into the room. All around them were huge pipes and glowing tanks that surrounded the reactors. Though the actual reactors were safe, about fifty metres further inside they could easily cripple the ship by removing the coolant and generator links from the rest of the ship. By Lieutenant Erdeniz's best calculations the reactor could manage three to four minutes once the link to its coolants supplies was removed. His plan was to overload the weapons grid at the same time. The strain should help to superheat the reactor and cause catastrophic damage.

A team of four engineers from the crew moved into the room, each of them carrying a crate of mining thermite charges. They were all experts at their jobs and it took less than a minute to rig the charges and set them with a three-minute timer. As Lieutenant Erdeniz set the timer the Corporal stopped him.

"You sure that's enough time for us to get out?"

"We can't take the chance, any less and they could get down here and disable the charges," replied the Lieutenant.

The marine nodded and helped the men to the corridor where they started to make their way back to the boats.

* * *

With a mighty flash all four entrances to the habitation zone lit up. The flash bangs were commonly used before an assault but not usually in this quantity. The Captain was taking no chances and as the dust settled, his unit charged through the gaps. The defending Zealots were momentarily taken by surprise and the marines were able to fight through the first line and work their way into the open area. Shots from above picked off a handful but their fire was not enough to hold back the tide. With the flash bangs being the signal, Spartan and his commandos rushed in from the rubble of the bar and moved into flanking positions. The expert marksmanship of the commandos quickly stopped the snipers and with their flanks protected, the rest moved in and targeted the Zealots guarding the civilians. A number of them turned on them, gunning down as many as they could before the marines were able to stop them. It was bloody work but luckily the commandos were fast and efficient and they were able to cut down the guards before too many of the civilians paid the price.

As the first groups were led to the safety of the landing shuttles and transports, Spartan and his squad kept pushing forward. A room at the end of the open space was showing on his scanner as holding a large number of people and he could hear screams coming from inside. Jesus made it first but as he ran inside a great shotgun blast blew him right back out of the door. His armoured suit protected him from the worst effects of the shot but it was still enough to put him out of the fight for a few seconds. Spartan pulled up next to the doorway and Teresa took the other side. He popped his head around the corner briefly and back again.

"Looks like three guys behind the table and about twenty to thirty hostages," he said over his radio.

"Drop your weapons, soldier, and come in!" came a voice from inside.

"Fuck you!" Spartan shouted.

"Do it, or we start shooting!" the man shouted back.

Spartan placed his weapon on the ground and slipped into the open, walking slowly into the room. As he entered he could see the three masked men, each wearing the armour and garb of the Zealots. They carried bladed weapons and one wore an explosive vest. In his hand he held a trigger device of some kind.

"Show us your hands!" shouted the man with the vest.

Spartan lifted his hands, pushing them forward so they could see them. In his right hand he held a flash grenade and in his left he held a detached pin. He tilted his left hand and the pin dropped to the floor. As the three men spotted the weapon, a look of fear spread over their eyes. The man stood to the right took a step back, pointing at the pin.

"Pick it up, do it now!"

Spartan leaned forward a little, looking for a moment as though he was complying. As he moved, the grenade dropped from his hand and started to roll towards the men. The man with the vest looked to his two comrades. Just as the grenade reached their feet it ignited, the bright flash filling the room and instantly blinding those without protection. As the men lifted their hands to protect their eyes, Spartan lowered his hand and pulled out his combat knife. With lightning fast reaction, he threw it ahead and struck the suicide bomber directly in the forehead. He slumped backwards, dead before he hit the ground. Spartan didn't wait though and leapt ahead, smashing his elbow into the second man. As his arm connected, Teresa entered the room with her L48 rifle raised to her shoulder. She fired two rounds into the third man's chest and then another to his head as he was blown backwards. She turned to her left in time to see Spartan snap the neck of the man. It was over as soon as it had started. He looked up at the group of crying civilians, they had been there weeks and looked terrified. Holding out his arm, he beckoned them to him. More commandos entered through the door and helped lead them out and to the waiting shuttles and transports.

"Captain, area secure, we're coming out," said Spartan with a feeling of satisfaction.

The fires were already spreading and as the last of the shuttles left a series of explosions ripped through the naval yard. By the time Spartan's shuttle reached a safe distance over half of the craft were already onboard the two marine transports. As usual, there was no sound as they moved away but it was clear from the smoke, fires and flashes that the surface of the Station was slowly being ripped apart from the inside. It was a selfish and cruel way to deny the Naval Station to the Confederation but at least they had eliminated the blockade and rescued most of the civilians. When the fires cleared, they would return and Titan would be rebuilt.

* * *

On board the Victorious the marines and crew fought their way to the outside of the ship as the remaining defenders tried to halt their progress. It was too little too late though, and as they reached the boats that could still move they boarded them and made their way back. Of the nearly five hundred marines and crew that had boarded the ship only three hundred and twelve made it back alive, the rest were killed, wounded or trapped on the massive vessel. As the last of the functioning boats left the ship, the thermite charge ignited.

The mining charges were a pyrotechnic composition of a metal powder and a metal oxide, which produce an exothermic oxidation-reduction reaction known as a thermite reaction. Though not explosive in the traditional sense they did produce short bursts of extremely high temperatures focused on a very small area for a short period of time.

As the incredible temperatures melted through the coolant pipes, they even managed to melt a section of the outer casing of the main reactor. It wasn't enough to cause a critical reaction but it did create a breach that sent deadly levels of radiation though the vessel. As the ship started to lose power, most of its weapon systems started to go offline as well as the docking couplers. In less than five minutes, the ship was powerless and drifting, its engines out of action and a deadly poison moving slowly through every section of the vessel.

* * *

Admiral Jarvis watched with satisfaction as the boats made their way back to the battlecruiser. With the couplers released, the two ships drifted apart though the debris and chunks of shattered metal still hung like a cloud between them. She turned to her XO.

"How many left?"

"Two more boats, they are leaving for the loading bays now, Admiral. One moment, okay, we are clear," he said.

"Get us out of here, fast!" she ordered.

With a great shudder the damaged but intact battlecruiser started to build up speed. As they reached the first kilometre away the first flashes from the rear quarter of the Victorious started to spread along sections of the old warship. A bright glow about a hundred metres from the stern of the battleship indicated the overloaded power core exploding. It was less than she expected but the results were exactly what she needed. Part of the hull tore away and the fires became worse as ammunition supplies and coolant mixed together. More explosions rocked the length of the ship, but no lifeboats were launched and no guns fired. The ship was far from destroyed, but she drifted like an ancient hulk with no signs of power or life to be seen.

"She's dead in space and still they won't leave her." The Admiral said quietly to herself.

Her XO stepped up, examining the tactical display. "It looks like the bulk of her crew are moving to this area on the ship, what do you think it is, some kind of escape vessel?" he asked.

"I don't know," replied the Admiral as she watched the screens. "Orbit at one hundred kilometres and load the guns, if she tries anything I want her finished, once and for all!"

CHAPTER TEN

The formation of the Zealots can be traced directly back to the great exodus of peoples following the Great War. What started as a political dispute quickly spread to trade and religion and involved every faction, company and colony. With the signing of the armistice and the formation of the Confederacy, many of the more extreme religious movements were forced to the frontiers or newly colonised planets. Though there was no official persecution there were many citizens who blamed religious groups for the violence in the later stages of the war. It was these disparate groups that found work in the quiet, dark places of the Confederation.

Origins of the Zealots

Spartan was absolutely exhausted. Every muscle in his body ached and his brain was pounding from the constant exertion and stress of the assault on Titan Naval Station. In the sealed environment of the shuttle, he could at least relax, but being strapped down into his seat was not ideal. Next to him was Jesus whilst Teresa was at the rear of the craft being tended by two of the onboard medics. Apparently, her injuries were serious but not critical. It was important however for them to remove her battle-damaged armour and attend to the wound directly. The emergency aid she had received during the battle had kept her in the fight but it was no substitute for actual medical care. From his view through the small windows on the flanks of the craft he could see the flickering lights of fires and explosions that were rattling through the hull of the battleship. News of the boarding actions and her crippling had spread through the boats and ships of the Fleet quickly as expected. As he watched the dying vessel in the far distance, he pulled himself back at the sight of the bright hull of the CCS Santa Maria. He had been so transfixed on the fires that the marine transport had almost appeared out of nowhere.

"Sergeant, we have an urgent transmission from Captain Mathews for you," came a voice over the boat's loudspeaker system.

"When it rains it pours, man!" said Jesus with a mischievous look.

Spartan leaned to his side and hit a button on the seat that activated the microphone system. He looked about the shuttlecraft, the eighteen marines were all part of the unit that had just escaped from the Station. Most had removed at least part of their armour but two still kept their helmets on, either because they were too tired and possibly because of the everlasting fear of all spacecraft-based infantry that they might end up in a vacuum without their sealed suits. The normally clean camouflaged armour they each wore was now scratched and burnt and many had streaks of blood from the battle on the moon.

"Captain Mathews, you're on loudspeaker. Are you onboard the Santa Maria?" he asked. There was a short pause before the speaker crackled and the Captain's familiar voice filled the craft.

"We're here, Sergeant, a damned fine piece of soldering there. The figures coming in are impressive, a lot of good people were saved down there," he said.

"A lot didn't make it back as well, Sir," replied Spartan.

"Very true and nobody will forget that, trust me. That is going to have to wait though. Right now I have an urgent job for your team and you're not going to like it," answered the Captain.

Jesus looked at Spartan and then back to the small number of sore and tired marines that were scattered about the craft. Some were injured, but none too seriously. They all looked like they could fall asleep at any moment.

"We're ready, what's the problem, Sir?" Spartan asked but he hesitated, almost not wanting to know what it was.

"A transport has managed to escape from the Victorious and was trying to make a dash out of the System. The Crusader was already moving away from the danger zone when she was spotted. Gunboats from CCS Wasp have already disabled her engines but she's now drifting towards Prime. With no propulsions, she can't pull away from the gravitational pull. We were going to leave her to burn up in the atmosphere, but we're picking up a large number of life signs on board. I know it's a risk but we can't take the chance until we know who is on board," he said.

"Zealots?" asked Jesus.

"Maybe, we estimate thirty to forty people and as far as we can tell they are the only people to make if off the Victorious."

"Interesting, it could be their command crew, maybe even senior members of the Zealots," Spartan said thoughtfully.

"Perhaps, Sergeant. But it could also be another hostage situation or even worse, some kind of a trap. I know your people have been through a lot but you're the last shuttle to get back. It will take another thirty minutes for us to get anybody else to the vessel. According to the computers, they will hit the atmosphere at about the same time. Your shuttle could do it in eight."

"Understood, we'll be there, Sir," Spartan answered.

"Thank you. Watch your backs and get back quickly. Spartan, when you're finished meet me on the Santa Maria, we have other business to discuss," he said before leaving.

Spartan was surprised by the last part of the message but the operation came first. He turned to the rest of the marines who had overheard the entire conversation. Two of the commandos were already loading rounds into their magazines.

"I know this is above and beyond, men."

"Not a problem," said one.

"Yeah, not like we've got anything else to do!" said another with a laugh.

"Ok, Jesus, can you get a tactical display up here so we can see what we're up against?" he asked.

Without getting up, Jesus took a computer tablet from the side of his seat and patched into the shuttle's systems. In just a few moments he brought up a three-dimensional model on the forward wall.

"Yeah, its a standard T9 armoured transport, the same kind of boat we use for transporting marines. It does look as if it's had some modifications," he said as he skimmed across its outline.

"What's that on the front?" asked one of the marines.

Spartan had already undone the straps holding him into his seat and was moving to his armour that was clipped into a mount on the wall. He moved to the front of the craft where the image was projected and looked closely, the section he was looking at was bigger than he had seen on the boats from the Santa Maria. He scratched his jaw as he tried to work out what it was. It wasn't just the nose, the entire vessel looked like it had been roughly bodged to do a particular job.

"I don't know. It might be extra armour. Anybody else know?"

"Wait, if you follow the line along the side you can see it is thicker all around the hull, I'd say she's been reinforced and sealed for some reason," said the marine.

"Sealed, as in from the inside or to keep us out?" asked Spartan. The marine shrugged.

"I don't like it. Either they have sealed it to keep something from getting out or they really don't want us going in," said Spartan.

"ETA three minutes," came the voice of the pilot over the speaker system.

Spartan looked back at the group and then the image of the craft before making up his mind.

"Well, we don't have the luxury of time. Here's the plan. First, we'll move alongside her and set up an airlock seal. We'll clamp down hard on her and make sure we've got a secure, pressurised access point to her cargo section. Next, I will lead a few armoured engineers in, that way if they have any surprises we'll be ready for them. They will have a very hard time damaging those units. The rest of you will follow and help secure the vessel. It is critical we maintain a solid seal, we don't want anyone dying in there, well, not until we find out who they are," he said with a smirk.

Spartan pulled himself along the craft until he reached the equipment section. There were three sets of engineer's armour mounted on the wall. Each was painted in dark grey, with the sharp edges of the digging tools painted in yellow and black stripes.

Spartan moved to the side, stepped into a suit and started clamping down the sections onto the mounts fitted to his personal protection suit. Though it added bulk to his body, it only increased his total size by about twenty percent. As he powered the system he twisted his right hand, checking the movement of the armoured hand and attached bulldozer type blades.

Jesus now reached him and started to attach the equipment on the second unit to his suit.

"If you go in with just the suits you'll have no weapons," said Peterson, one of the commandos who had fought alongside them on the Station.

Spartan activated his left arm and swung it in front of him, the edges on the digger blade were the size of man's torso. "I always have these!" he said with a wicked grin.

"Yeah, I heard about some crazy guy using them during training, let me guess who that was," he laughed.

"Have you used one before?"

"Of course, Spartan, combat engineering is a required course for all advanced commando recruits. You'd know that if you did the full training," he said sarcastically.

As the three prepared their equipment Teresa pulled herself along the side of the craft to them. She was still not wearing her armour and once they started the boarding action she'd have to stay in one of the pressurised compartments in case of any breaches.

"Spartan," she said. He turned around, only just avoiding hitting her with one of the heavy blades.

"How are you doing now, Teresa?" he asked.

"Not great, Spartan, the medics say I'll need surgery to fix my shoulder. Part of the bone is shattered and the tissue needs work. I'll live though."

She reached out and put her hand on the thickly reinforced armour around Spartan's shoulder.

"Just watch yourself in there, I'll see you on the ship," she said and then pulled herself back.

As she moved to the safety of the emergency pressurised compartments, Spartan did final checks on his equipment. The last thing he wanted was a poorly fitted strap or plate to fail in what could be a major combat operation.

The shuttle slowed as the pilot adjusted their course. With expert skill, he spun them around so that the access hatches on the right of the shuttle faced the matching points on the other craft. It was a delicate manoeuvre as both craft were now spinning slowly as they moved ever closer to the outer orbit of the planet. One incorrect move and the two craft could collide and even at a relatively slow speed could cause damage. The other problem was that they were now perilously close to the outer atmosphere of Proxima Prime. If they suffered any kind of technical problems, they would face the same fate of the transport, a quick and fiery journey as they were cooked alive.

"You'll have six minutes, no more and then we're gone. Don't be late!" said the pilot as they bumped gently into position.

For a few seconds a dull vibration hammered around the craft as the magnetic seal was created. A series of metal brackets pushed out and fixed them to the outer skin of the transport, the link was strong and only a power failure on the shuttle could pull them apart. A flexible tube extended from the shuttle to the doorway on the transport and affixed itself around the door. As the pumps started up the tube pressurised and a link was formed. With the airtight seal ready, the final task was normalising pressure and opening the door. It took just seconds as the experienced marines bypassed the outer security door and cut the seals on the inner door, opening up access to the loading bay of the vessel.

The inside of the vessel was pitch dark though the marines couldn't tell if it was intentional or simply down to power failure. Spartan switched on his lighting and the two shoulder-mounted lamps lit up the area in front. Inside it seemed to be full of a light mist that shifted and spread through the airlock. With the powerful lamps burning through the mist they looked like yellow beams that were seeking prey. For a moment Spartan worried it might be a kind of weapon and was about to hit his alarm button for the shuttle crew. His fears were averted however when he spotted one of the damaged generators for the landing gear on the boat. From the cracks along its length the same mist pumped out slowly, it was probably damage sustained during the craft's escape from the burning battleship. Feeling a little more relaxed his spoke though his intercom to the rest of the marines and the crew on the shuttle.

"The doorway is secure, no obvious power in the transport. Engineers follow me, marines wait until we have cleared the first section," he said.

He took a step forward and his grav boots clunked down on the metallic surface. Each step he made triggered a small light in his helmet that told him whether he was attached to the surface or not. It had been drummed in to him to ensure one light was always on, indicating that he had one foot anchored at all times. So far, everything looked safe. As he continued onwards, he constantly moved his lamps to check every dark corner. The small lights were mounted on a motorised pintle that allowed them to rotate in any direction. As he moved his eyes, the sensors in his helmet followed his retinas and moved the lamps accordingly. From inside the suit it gave the impression that the lights came directly from his eyes.

"Loading bay is clear, I'm now moving on to the

passenger section."

As Spartan moved slowly forward, Jesus and Peterson followed. Their engineer's armour was bulky and slow, but they provided plenty of cover for the rest of the conventionally armoured marines to enter the craft behind them. At the end of the loading bay was a large metal blast door. To the side of the door there was a panel and a series of buttons. He moved to touch it when Peterson's hand blocked him.

"Sorry, Sergeant, you don't want to press that one, it's the cargo access panel. The passenger panel is this one," he said.

The marine pushed a button on the much lower panel and with a shudder the large metal door started to lift upwards. The speed was slow and Spartan took a step back in case anything came out from the gap to grab at them. As he moved back, he lowered his arms, the sharp blades waiting for anything to appear.

"Marines, hold your fire, watch for hostiles!" ordered Spartan.

The three at the front lowered their arms and pushed the sharp digging blades in front of them. Around the three armoured suits a number of the other marines pushed though the gaps, each one holding up their L48 carbines and rifles. After a few more seconds, the door thumped into position and revealed the large passenger area. It was designed to carry hundreds of passengers though there were no signs of people yet.

"I can see nothing. Anybody else?" asked Jesus.

"Wait, what's this?" asked Spartan as he took a few steps forward.

Several metres inside the craft were a number of crates and containers. They were stacked two or three high and filled nearly half of the entire open space. They were all strapped in with a series of thick straps, ropes and chains and gave the impression they had been loaded in a hurry. Some of them were damaged and a few of the larger ones were open. A first Spartan thought they reminded him of coffins but then he spotted the symbols on the side. Moving closer he checked the details, the first one was from a medical centre on Prime.

"Sarge!" shouted one of the marines, as several shadows flickered across the wall to the right.

Jesus tried to track the movement but they were too fast and disappeared behind one of the crates. He checked on his helmet-mounted display and picked up two more shapes but again, by the time he had them in his sights they vanished behind the crates.

"Did anybody see that?" asked Peterson.

Before anyone could answer one of the larger crates ripped open and a man-shaped object tumbled out towards the marines. Spartan stared in fascination at what looked like a flailing man as he drifted weightlessly towards them. He looked at him carefully and quickly realised the man was simply drifting, there were no signs of life or movement from him.

"What the hell?" shouted one of the marines.

As the body drifted towards them Spartan pushed out his armoured arms and caught the body. He pulled it closer towards him, examining it in fascinated detail.

"I don't get it, it is a man but look at his hands and face," he said.

Jesus and three of the other marines moved closer. Expanded and grotesque muscles distorted his limbs but his skull appeared thicker and extended. The man's jaw bulged to the rear and scars ran down his cheeks. Spartan looked at his hand and noticed the thick, powerful fingers and a series of serrated blades attached to the back of the arm that extended out and past the fingers. It was like some kind of bizarre experiment that had fused weapons and a mutated beast. They looked in some of the damaged crates and could see more of the bodies.

"I've got movement," said Peterson.

He took a step to the side, making room for more of the marines to enter. The lightly armoured marines filled the gaps and scanned the area, each holding up their firearms and looking for anything remotely hostile.

"Okay, this isn't good, patch me through to Captain Mathews," said Spartan as he spoke directly to the pilot of the shuttle.

"Mathews here, what have you found?" asked the

officer.

"I don't know, Sir. There are bodies here but they are distorted or changed in some way. The crates say they are from bio labs on Prime. One of them is from a military base on Kerberos, how the hell did they get like that?"

"Distorted in what way?" asked a concerned Captain Mathews.

"The muscles are thicker, the neck and jaw are enlarged and the body here has scars down the face. They are all wearing some kind of reinforced plating, it looks almost like crude armour, Sir," he explained.

"Armour? I don't like it, get your people out of there, now!" he shouted.

Spartan stared intently at the body, trying to ascertain what madness could have created such a thing. As he looked at his face he noticed the eyes, both were bloodshot and staring straight ahead. Then he remembered, the eyes were closed a moment before. As the realisation dawned on him, the grotesque man reached and grabbed at Spartan's face.

"Fuck!" he screamed as he staggered backwards and crashed into the wall. More of the shapes started to move and before Spartan could even try to straighten himself the creatures were all over the marines.

Jesus pushed himself forward, trying to stem the assault but there were simply too many of them. One crawled over his armour and then repeatedly stabbed at his helmet with a piece of twisted metal. The first strike jarred his head and the subsequent strikes forced him to lose his footing and drift inside the craft. He waved his left arm, desperately trying to knock the crazy man from his armour.

The regular marines opened fire where they could, each burst of fire ripping into the rough armour of the enemy. The metal absorbed much of the impact, but the marines' fire was accurate and continuous. Four of the creatures were killed outright, but their wounded kept coming. One spun off the ceiling and swung both of its arms as it tried to hack at the marines. One of its blades took a chunk out of a marine's face as the second became stuck in another's chest.

Peterson, seeing the terrible carnage all around, stomped forward and using his armoured digging tools on his arms managed to cut a swathe through the group. One flew from the wall and grabbed at his right arm. He took three steps and then crushed it hard against the side of the transport. It howled and released him long enough for his right fist to force his blade deep into the thing's throat. Blood pumped out and drifted in thick blobs through the boat.

Spartan pushed himself up, slamming his metal arm hard into his attacker.

"Marines, back to the shuttle!" he cried.

As they retreated the creatures continued their attack,

each one biting, tearing and hacking at anything they could reach. Jesus and three marines were struggling under a mass of the creatures and Spartan tried desperately to reach him. One marine was cut clean in half right before him and another was tossed aside like a rag. He grabbed Jesus and yanked him away from the mass of blood and gore. One of them tried to grab at his face but Spartan's left arm held its neck and neatly snapped it in two. He looked back at Jesus, noting the holes and damage across the armour. He kept moving back towards the access hatch with the surviving commandos provided covering fire. As they fell back into the shuttle one of the marines hit the large red seal button on the wall and the airlock doors slammed down.

Spartan staggered two more paces and then stopped. His breathing was laboured and his armour was splattered in blood, though how much was theirs and how much belonged to the marines he didn't know.

"We're clear!" he shouted into his intercom.

The pilot was obviously waiting for the signal and in seconds they had broken free and were accelerating from the transport and its deadly crew.

As Spartan pulled himself out of his armour, Teresa grabbed him.

"Are you okay, are you hurt?" she asked in a desperate tone.

"I'm fine, don't worry," he said as he looked at the

pitiful remnants of the mission.

"A lot of us didn't come back," he said in a grim tone.

Teresa searched the faces of the marines who had made it back.

"Where is Jesus?" she cried. Spartan simply turned his head.

* * *

In the medical bay of the Santa Maria scores of marines were undergoing emergency medical aid. Teresa was on one of the examination beds while a medic examined her shoulder.

"You were very lucky, the aid pack stopped the bleeding and the bone is only partially damaged. I've applied a temporary seal and the pins will need to stay in until the tissue sealant kicks in. You'll need to return in thirty-six hours for me to remove the pins," she said before turning to wave another injured marine forward.

Teresa stood up and Spartan helped her put her jacket back on.

"How are you feeling?"

"I've been better, it could be a lot worse though," she replied.

The two walked along the main corridor and into the mess hall to find mass celebrations going on. News of the final victories had spread through the ships and it was clearly going down well. Two more cruisers had just arrived and the rumour was that army transports wouldn't be far behind. After hours of bloody combat, both in space and on the stations, the battle was finally over. With the civilians rescued, the Fleet had moved into a high orbit and established a strong blockade over the planet.

Spartan was moving ahead and towards the marines when he spotted Captain Mathews and a few of the commands chatting near a computer terminal. The officer quickly spotted Spartan and waved him over. The two walked over as the din from the rest of the marines continued in the background.

"How is the shoulder, Private?" Captain Mathews asked Teresa.

"It is pretty stiff. They will be looking at it tomorrow, right now they've got many more serious injuries to deal with. It's not life threatening, just a real bitch!" she said.

"Glad to hear that," he said before turning to Spartan.

"I'm sorry about your boarding party, it was a tough call but we had to know who was on board. How many of you got back?" he asked with a concerned look.

"I lost seven marines back there plus the rest have got a variety of wicked injuries. I don't know what those things were but they came from somewhere and nothing would stop them, Sir," he said quietly.

Captain Mathews was watching the marine's camera feeds on his tablet as Spartan continued to talk. The picture was fuzzy and showed little detail on the attackers as they moved constantly in the darkness.

"Well, we've been hearing rumours from Prime about various things going on at the Bone Mill as well as other Zealot strongholds through the Confederation. It's a shame you weren't able to bring any of them back for study. Still, your video feeds will be better than nothing."

"Better than nothing? What the..." Teresa shouted, but Spartan lifted his arm, gently keeping her away from the officer.

"That wasn't the way I meant it, I have nothing but respect for the tremendous work and sacrifice you have all given. You have done the Corps and your unit proud. I've recommended you all to the General and I know he has something big planned.." he said before being interrupted.

"Have you seen the news?" shouted a marine as he ran past.

Teresa turned and watched him join a growing number of the crowd clustered around the large screens in the hall. Each screen was several metres wide and could be seen from halfway down the room. The sound in the room started to drop as more of the marines quietened, each of them enthralled by the video feeds.

"Come on," said Spartan.

He moved off to examine the large screens and whatever news was getting all the attention. Teresa, Captain Mathews and the rest of the commandos followed him.

As they reached the screens they stopped, each of them too busy watching to speak.

The screens were showing three repeating feeds, all of them from ground units in the trenches around the Bone Mill. A voice running over the top explained the material had been received in the last hour. The first screen shook quite badly and it was evident that the camera was mounted on a soldier somewhere. From the view, a group of five soldiers stood chatting when a series of explosions blurred the view. As the feed refocused and the dust cleared the other soldiers were getting up off the ground, though the man carrying the camera must have been hurt or killed as the camera remained stationary and on its side. A series of streaks moved past the camera and one of the soldiers waved his arms before a large number of hooded figures leapt into the trench. Each of the figures carried evil looking edged weapons and proceeded to slash and hack at the soldiers. Only one of them managed to get off a shot before he was knocked down and decapitated right in front of the camera.

An audible gasp rushed through the group of marines as they watched the Confederation soldiers being cut down in such a brutal and callous way. More Confed troops moved into the trench to try and retake it but even though they slaughtered dozens of the enemy, sheer weight of numbers pushed them back until the video feed showed nothing but crowds of the hooded, sinister figures.

They started to chatter when the second feed showed the terrible scale of what was happening. The feed said it was from an aerial reconnaissance drone directly above the Bone Mill. All around the perimeter a series of flashes and explosions signalled the start of the assault. From all across the structure swarms of the men came out in a bloody charge. The camera zoomed in to show at least ten of them leaping past soldiers as they were firing weapons and hacking with axes and blades.

The final feed was from a fixed camera mount on a vehicle near the battle. As the attackers moved in the camera zoomed in and paused on a group of three of them. The nearest one was biting into the shoulder of a soldier and another was in the middle of cutting down a fleeing civilian. Both were wearing a motley collection of metal plated armour that covered various parts of the body. It wasn't pretty but certainly did the job of making them look terrible and dangerous.

"What the fuck is that?" shouted one of the watching marines.

"Zealot bastards!" shouted another.

Spartan was in shock, the attackers were exactly the same as the ones he had just been fighting on the transport. He turned to the Captain who was transfixed by the screens.

"Sir, that is what we found on the transport. They are strong, really strong and they can take a lot of punishment. Those soldiers aren't going to stand a chance," he said.

Captain Mathews reached down and pulled out his tablet. He looked at it, whatever he saw drained the blood from his face and within a few seconds he was already moving away from them.

"I need to go, Sergeant, we'll be in touch," he said before rushing off along with his group of commandos.

Spartan and Teresa looked at each other, before they could speak the loudspeakers throughout the hall burst into noise.

"This is Admiral Jarvis. Congratulations on an excellent operation. I can confirm that the stations have been neutralised and Confed forces are back in control of this sector!" she said. There was a short pause before she continued but in a much slower and more sombre tone.

"As you have probably heard, a massive and coordinated planet-wide offensive has begun on the surface of Prime. Initial reports say over ten thousand fighters have already broken out from the Bone Mill and more are appearing from underground facilities across the surface. We do not have clear information on the attackers but they have already overrun three army barracks and one marine brigade is conducting a fighting withdrawal to the Carlos spaceport. Infantry reinforcements are due to arrive in three hours. The marine battle group is being placed in reserve whilst it is re-equipped and re-supplied at the Kerberos naval yard. The rest of the Fleet will maintain the blockade around Prime and provide humanitarian assistance where required."

More feeds from the planet showed the terrible carnage the horribly altered, or mutated, people were causing. They used firearms but when they were close enough they seemed to delight in using edged weapons and even worse, they were able and willing to use their hands and teeth to literally tear people apart. It was foul and sickening and an enemy that made the Zealots pale into insignificance.

Teresa turned to Spartan as the marines around them erupted in excited shouting and arguments. "What the hell are they?"

Spartan said nothing. He just stood there dumbfounded. He couldn't believe that there were more of those things still around. Based on the massive strength and capacity for absorbing damage he could already see the threat they posed. Finally he spoke.

"They must be a new weapon the Zealots have been working on, they are stronger and more dangerous than any man I've had to face, we've got a big, big problem."

A marine officer pushed through the throng of people, handing out papers before reaching Spartan, he looked at Teresa and then back to Spartan.

"Sergeant Spartan?" he asked. Spartan nodded, saying nothing.

"I have papers from Captain Mathews. It says you are to join these marines on the Santa Cruz as part of the new Commando Company. You need to be fast, they are shipping out in twenty minutes."

"Commando Company, what about me?" asked Teresa.

The officer showed her the list, she spotted her name on the paper. "That's me," she said.

"Ah, yeah, it says you're to go too, you need to report to your new commander when you get to the Cruz," he said before turning to head back to the mass of marines.

"Wait!" shouted Teresa as she grabbed the officer's arm. He turned but looked flustered at being grabbed.

"Which commander?" she demanded.

"Um, General Rivers, he is taking command of the ship for something special. Don't ask me what, I've no idea," he said as Teresa made to interrupt him.

"That's it?" Spartan asked him.

"He'll tell you more when you get there I'm sure," he said before finally turning and rushing off.

"General Rivers, why is he in charge of one ship, Spartan?"

"Who knows, we'd better hurry though or we'll never find out!" said Spartan as they made their way to the transport level and the waiting shuttle. Scores of marines were already on board and they had to queue just to get on. After a short wait they climbed aboard and headed to their designated positions. Spartan noticed many more marines rushing about on the Santa Maria, some were heading to their quarters and others went to waiting shuttles.

"I thought this was over, we've done enough fighting

to last a whole career!" Teresa said as she buckled herself into her seat.

Spartan turned his head in disagreement as he pulled the harness down tightly.

"No chance, this is just the start, and from what I've seen it is about to get very bloody," he said with a grimace.

"All crew to their stations, we leave for the Santa Cruz in sixty seconds," the pilot announced over the loudspeaker system.

The crew were already closing the door and going through the safety procedures prior to leaving the main hangar section of the ship. From inside the shuttle Spartan couldn't see outside into space yet, but he could see several of the other shuttles preparing to leave. One of them must have just arrived from one of the warships, as it brought dozens of injured marines sprawled out on bloody stretchers. The marine transports seemed to be able to do just about everything.

For a brief moment Spartan felt a pang as he realised that he was leaving his home but then he remembered what it was actually like inside. He could manage without it. Teresa smiled at him, noticing he was lost in his thoughts, before lightly thumping his arm.

"I bet you're wondering about your decision to join up now right?" she asked him.

Spartan thought back to the courtroom and the choice he had made. Right now, he wasn't so sure on his decision.

Still, it wouldn't be long before his first year was up, only nine more to go.

"Well, I wasn't, but now you've got me thinking about it!" he said with a mischievous look.

THE END

CPSIA information can be obtained at www.ICGtesting.com
Printed in the USA
LVOW130258061112

306030LV00002B/1/P